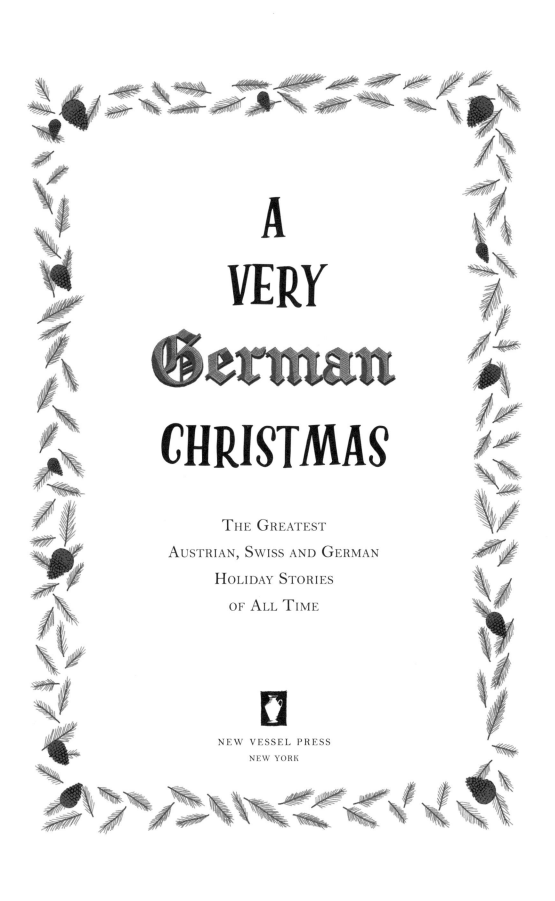

A VERY German CHRISTMAS

THE GREATEST
AUSTRIAN, SWISS AND GERMAN
HOLIDAY STORIES
OF ALL TIME

NEW VESSEL PRESS
NEW YORK

New Vessel Press

www.newvesselpress.com

Library of Congress Cataloging-in-Publication Data
Various
A Very German Christmas: The Greatest Austrian, Swiss and German Holiday Stories of All Time /
various authors.
p. cm.
ISBN 978-1-939931-88-7
Library of Congress Control Number 2020935345
I. Austria, Switzerland, Germany—Fiction

Table of Contents

✳

A
VERY
German
CHRISTMAS

THE ELVES AND THE SHOEMAKER

The Brothers Grimm

There was once a shoemaker, who worked very hard and was very honest, but still he could not earn enough to live upon; and at last all he had in the world was gone, save just leather enough to make one pair of shoes.

Then he cut his leather out, all ready to make up the next day, meaning to rise early in the morning to his work. His conscience was clear and his heart light amid all his troubles; so he went peaceably to bed, left all his cares to Heaven, and soon fell asleep. In the morning after he had said his prayers, he sat himself down to his work; when, to his great wonder, there stood the shoes already made, upon the table. The good man knew not what to say or think at such an odd thing happening. He looked at the workmanship; there was not one false stitch in the whole job; all was so neat and true, that it was quite a masterpiece.

The same day a customer came in, and the shoes suited him so well that he willingly paid a price higher than usual for them; and the poor shoemaker, with the money, bought leather enough to make two pairs more. In the evening he cut out the work, and went to bed early, that he might get up and begin betimes next day; but he was saved all the trouble, for when he got up in the morning the work was done ready to his hand. Soon in came buyers, who paid him handsomely for his goods, so that he bought leather enough for four pair more. He cut out the work again overnight and found it done in the morning, as before; and so it went on for some time: what was got ready in the evening was always done by daybreak, and the good man soon became thriving and well off again.

One evening, about Christmastime, as he and his wife were sitting over the fire chatting together, he said to her, "I should like to sit up and watch tonight, that we may see who it is that comes and does my work for me." The wife liked the thought; so they left a light burning, and hid themselves in a corner of the room, behind a curtain that was hung up there, and watched what would happen.

As soon as it was midnight, there came in two little naked dwarfs; and they sat themselves upon the shoemaker's bench, took up all the work that was cut out, and began to ply with their little fingers, stitching and rapping and tapping away at such a rate, that the shoemaker was all wonder, and could not take his eyes off them. And on they went, till the job was quite done, and the shoes stood ready for use upon the table. This was long before daybreak; and then they bustled away as quick as lightning.

The next day the wife said to the shoemaker, "These little wights have made us rich, and we ought to be thankful to them, and do them a good turn if we can. I am quite sorry to see them run about as they do; and indeed it is not very decent, for they have nothing upon their backs to keep off the cold. I'll tell you what, I will make each of them a shirt, and a coat and waistcoat, and a pair of pantaloons into the bargain; and do you make each of them a little pair of shoes."

The thought pleased the good cobbler very much; and one evening, when all the things were ready, they laid them on the table, instead of the work that they used to cut out, and then went and hid themselves, to watch what the little elves would do.

About midnight in they came, dancing and skipping, hopped around the room, and then went to sit down to their work as usual; but when they saw the clothes lying for them, they laughed and chuckled, and seemed mightily delighted.

Then they dressed themselves in the twinkling of an eye, and danced and capered and sprang about, as merry as could be; till at last they danced out at the door, and away over the green.

The good couple saw them no more; but everything went well with them from that time forward, as long as they lived.

1806

AFTER CHRISTMAS

Hermann Hesse

In the days after the Christmas festivities, I uneasily eyed a few packages that were lying around on top of my chest of drawers and causing me to worry. These were things I received as gifts but for which I had no need and that now had to be exchanged. This is how it's always done, and it's astonishing that after the Christmas rush the saleswomen in nice shops manage to spare so much good cheer for the days of gift returns. Nonetheless, I don't like doing these errands. Shopping is difficult enough for me, and I tend to put it off—and now to make exchanges, to go into the stores, to deal with people, and once again take an interest in matters that have already been dealt with! No, I can't stand it, and if it were left solely up to me, I would simply put the unusable gifts in a drawer, and leave them there forever.

Luckily my lady friend understands these things quite well, and I asked her to accompany me to three shops. She did so happily, not just to please me, but also because it was fun for her, it was a kind of sport, a kind of art that gave her joy. So we went together to the glove shop, where we greeted everyone, unwrapped my Christmas gloves, and I, fidgeting nervously with my hat in my hand, sought just the right manner of speech with which one customarily undertakes such transactions, but I didn't quite succeed and so let my helper do the talking. And sure enough, the magic flowed, they smiled, they took back—thank God—the gloves, and suddenly I stood before an array of colorful shirts and was allowed to choose one of them. That suited me, so I played the expert, recalling after some thought my collar size, and soon, carrying a new package, we left the shop, where in the aftermath of celebrating the Savior's birth one can now spend an entire day exchanging walking sticks, gloves, and hats.

It went equally well with the new fountain pen. I had to press into a crowded store, perch in front of a pleasant young woman, receive writing paper and several pens to select from, and while seated there I wrote and drew flowers, stars, and initials on a page until it was full. I left with one of the pens I had tried out, and then if writing were to still prove tiresome for me, it could not be the fault of the pen; it's a golden pen from America, one fills it with a golden lever, and golden words stream joyfully forth. But I need it more for drawing. Gratefully I put the small golden creation with its golden tip into my bag and went on, trudged to the optician, to whom I had to confess that my new reading glasses didn't serve me well and that he should take them back and make a new pair. Shielded by my lady friend, emboldened by my success with the shirt and the pen, I entered purposefully into this glazed realm, was listened to, and indeed the good man took back my glasses. I never would have believed it. I myself wouldn't have done it in his place.

The victory lap through the three dreaded stores, the trek in the cold winter wind with my friend, the transformation of three embarrassing packages into three delightful ones was reason enough to render me chipper and grateful. As part of the exchange of the gloves, I even managed to obtain a compact pocket mirror that I was able to present as a gift to my escort.

On the way home I was very pleased and wanted to get back to work, to deal with all the unread letters that had piled up over the last days. I recalled my childhood and how the days after Christmas were so beautiful, with every morning's awakening and every return home involving the reward of new gifts and rejoicing in their possession. Once I received a violin, and even woke up in the middle of the night to touch it and gently pluck the strings. Once I was given *Don Quixote*, and every stroll or walk to church, even every meal was an unpleasant interruption from my blissful reading.

This time I hadn't received such thrilling things. The violin, the book, the toy, the skates no longer offer such splendor and magic to old people. Three boxes of good cigars stood there—that was reassuring—and some wine and cognac with which I could while away the evening. The new fountain pen was nice, but it was ill-suited for holding close to my heart and indulging in the delight of ownership.

There was however one thing, one gift, that was truly worth celebrating, truly extraordinary and magical, that one could take out in quiet moments, rapturously inspect, that you could look at and fall in love with. I took it out and sat by the window. It was, beautifully mounted under glass, a splendid exotic butterfly that went by the name of Urania and came from Madagascar. The beautifully built creature with slender, powerful wings and a rich scalloped pattern underneath floated gently on a branch, its upper body striped green and black and with rust-red hairs below and its tiny head gleaming golden green. The upper wings were patterned in green-and-black, and on the visible side a splendid warm and golden glowing green, but on the back side a very cool, tender silver sprinkled Veronese green, in which the crystalline wing ribs shimmered nobly. The underwing, however, fantastically jagged, displayed aside from the green and black pattern, a large gleaming field of deep gold, that in the light seemed almost copper red, even scarlet, whimsically covered with dark black patches, and at the bottom, the butterfly was, like the hem of a woman's gown, trimmed with a fine blend of short blond-and-black fur. Besides this the underwing had another special quality and characteristic: it was traversed by a short, dreamy zigzag line of pure white that dissolved to some extent into the entire wing, and made it into a loose play of air and gold dust and appeared to forcefully repel fantastic beam-like rays. There was something splendidly mysterious and kindly about this Madagascan butterfly, this airy African dream of green, black, and gold that could not be found on Christmas tables anywhere else in the city. To return to this was a joy, to immerse oneself in its presence a celebration.

For a long time, I sat bent over this stranger from Madagascar and let it enchant me. In many ways it reminded me, in many ways it admonished me, it spoke to me of many things. It was the image of beauty, the image of fortune, the image of art. Its form was a victory over death, its play of colors a smile of superiority over impermanence. It was a unique, beaming smile, this preserved dead butterfly under glass, a smile of many sorts, appearing variously as childish to me, then ancient and wise, soon combatively shaking, then painfully mocking—beauty always smiles this way, so smile all creations in which life appears to have permanently curdled, the beauty that has become a perpetually flowing form, whether it be a flower or an animal, an Egyptian head or the death mask of a genius. It was superior and eternal, this smile, and it was, when one lost oneself in it, suddenly ghostly wild and crazy, it was beautiful and cruel, tender and dangerous, full of paramount reason and full of the wildest folly. Wherever life for an instant appears to be fully formed, it has this contradictory aspect. There is no great music that doesn't at times seem to us like childish laughter and then at others like the deepest grief. Beauty is always like that everywhere: a lovely mirrored surface beneath which chaos lies in wait. Fortune is always like that everywhere: gleaming for a magical instant and then fading again, blown away by the breath of the death imperative. This is high art, the lofty wisdom of the select forever and everywhere: smiling knowingly into the abyss, assenting to suffering, and the play of harmony amid the eternal death throes of contradictions.

The fleeting purple could be sweetly glanced amid the golden splendor, the dark black-and-green marks tautly stretched over the wing ribs, with the slender spikes of color playfully sending out sparks. You lovely guest, you enchanting alien! Did you fly from Madagascar specially to fill my winter evening with a colorful dream? Did you run away from the paint box of the eternal mother just to sing me an old song of wisdom about the unity of contradictions, to teach me again what I already so often knew and have so often forgotten? Did a patient human hand so neatly preserve you and glue you on your branch, so that for a lonely hour a sick man would be enchanted with your sparkling playfulness, to console himself with your silent dreams? Were you killed and put under glass so that your eternal suffering and dying could console us, so the immortal suffering and dying of the great sufferer, curiously beloved and comforting to the true artist, could instead lift our souls from their desperation?

Evening light plays palely over your shimmering golden wings, slowly the red gold dissolves and soon all the magic, enveloped by darkness, can no longer be seen. But still the game of eternity is continually playing itself out, the brave artist's game of the endurance of beauty—the song plays on in my soul, in my thoughts the colorful rays continue to flicker with life. The poor beautiful butterfly didn't die in vain in Madagascar, the anxious hand didn't preserve its wing and antennae so carefully and lastingly for nothing. This tiny embalmed pharaoh will bear witness to me about its empire of the sun for a long time to come, and when it has long since disintegrated and I too am long gone, then somewhere in some soul something of its blissful play and wise smile will flourish and continue to be passed along, just as the gold of Tutankhamun still gleams today, and the blood of the Savior still flows in our time.

1928

BERLIN AT CHRISTMASTIDE

Heinrich Heine

This year we have had very little snow, and consequently we have scarcely heard the sleigh bells and the cracking of whips. As in all great Protestant towns, Christmastide plays the chief part in the great winter comedies. One week beforehand everyone is busy purchasing Christmas presents. All the costume shops and all the jewelry and hardware merchants make display of their choicest articles as our dandies do their learned acquaintances. On the Sc.hlossplatz are erected a crowd of wooden stalls hung with clothing, household goods and toys, and the sprightly Berliners flit like butterflies from shop to shop, buy, gossip, ogle, and show their taste and themselves at the same time, to admiring onlookers. But it is in the evening that the fun is at its height; for then these charmers, often with the whole of their respective families, with father, mother, aunt, brothers, and sisters, are to be seen, pilgrimaging from one confectioner's stall to another, as though to the stations of the cross. These dear folks pay their two groschen for entrance money, they feast their eyes to their heart's content on the exhibition, on a lot of dolls made of sugar or of comfits, which are displayed tastefully one beside the other. Lighted round about, and stored within four walls painted in perspective, they form a pretty enough picture. The amusing point of the thing is that these sugar puppets frequently represent some real and well-known personage.

I wandered through a crowd of these confectioners' booths, for I know nothing more diverting than to watch unobserved, how the pretty Berliners enjoy themselves, how their bosoms swell with excitement, palpitate rapidly, and how these naive souls ejaculate shrilly, "Ah, but it is lovely!" At Fuch's, during the exhibition this year, were to be seen pictures of Lalla Rookh such as were shown last year at the castle during the court festival of which you have heard. It was impossible for me to see anything of these wonders at Fuch's, because the pretty heads of these ladies formed an impenetrable wall before the square sugar tableau. I will not bore you with my opinion of this confectioners' exhibition; on it Karl Müchler, the war minister, he who, it is said, is the Berlin correspondent of the *Elegante Welt*, has already written an article in that paper.

1822

CHRISTMAS

Kurt Tucholsky

Thus standing 'fore the German rubble
I meekly sing my Christmas song.
I'll neither heed nor need to trouble
with all the wide world's right and wrong.
That's for others. Laid upon us.
I hum so soft, the sound near gone,
that tune with all its youthful promise:
O Tannenbaum!

Were I Knecht Ruprecht spreading blessings
and saw this pandemonium
—the Germans have no use for lessons—
God knows! I'd turn the way I'd come.
The last of the breadcorn's falling, blighted.
The alleys bare their teeth and foam.
I'd drape them from your boughs delighted,
O Tannenbaum!

I stare into the candles crackling:
Who holds the guilt that runs so deep?
Who threw us into blood, and cackling?

CHRISTMAS

Us Germans, patient as the sheep?
They do not mourn. They man their station.
I dreamt my dream I thought was gone
Close off and cease their arrogation!
Ignore the scoundrels' cruel predation!
Then sing with Christmas liberation:
O Tannenbaum! O Tannenbaum!

1918

INTERVIEW WITH SANTA CLAUS

Erich Kästner

The doorbell was ringing again. The ninth time in the last hour! Today, it seemed, every doorbell lover in the city was out. Such days do occur. I shuffled off grumpily toward the door and opened it.

Who, if you can believe it, stood outside? Saint Nicholas himself! In his famed historic outfit. White beard and rosy cheeks. The sack of apples, nuts, and gingerbread over his shoulder. The stern hazel switch in his gentle hand.

"Oh!" I said. "Nicholas the stressed!"

"Nicholas the *blessed*, if you please. *B* and *l*." He sounded a little irritated.

"As a boy I always called you 'Nicholas the stressed.' I found that more plausible."

"That was *you?*"

"So you remember, then?"

"Of course! You were a cute little rascal back then!"

"I'm still little."

"And you live here now."

"That's right."

We smiled resignedly and thought on times past. Then he suddenly recalled his Christmas duties and asked, as a businesslike aside: "Were the children nice this year? Who was naughty, and how so?"

I clarified for him that I keep a childless household, and am too fond of children to over-burden them by acting as their father.

"Lazybones!" he growled, and turned to leave the landing.

"But stay awhile!" I begged him. "Drink a cup of coffee with me!" To be frank, I felt sorry for him. This wintry life of delivering packages, up and down staircase after staircase, and over and over the stereotypical, slightly foolish inquiries after the good or bad behavior of beloved children, who feared him and froze in their prayers at the thought of him—this was a job fundamentally unsuitable for a reasonably-educated, thousand-year-old man. "Do me the honor!" I continued. "There's raisin bread."

What can I tell you? He stayed. He deigned to stay. First he wiped his boots clean on the doormat, then he leaned his sack against the coatrack, hung the switch on one of its hooks, and finally drank a cup of coffee with me in the sitting room. With it he ate four pieces of raisin bread. Thick slices. Pola, the small black cat, had sprung onto his shoulders at the second slice, and was now lying like a fur boa around his neck and purring. The sound was like that of a gnome seated at a sewing machine.

"You keep a cozy place here," he said. "Decidedly comfortable."

"Would you care for a cigar?"

"I wouldn't turn one down."

I offered the box. He helped himself. I gave him a light. Then with a sigh of relief he pulled off his right boot with the help of his left. "It's the support for my flat foot. It puts a cruel pressure on the bottom of my foot."

"You poor man! With *your* job!"

"There's less work these days. Good thing for my feet. These phony Nicholases shoot up like mushrooms from the ground. Wherever you look, they stumble through the streets and squares by the dozen."

"On the other hand—one day the children will believe that you, the true Santa Claus, no longer exist!"

"True! The scoundrels damage my reputation! Most of them, who throw on a fur, hang a beard off their faces, and copy me, don't have the least talent! They bungle it! It's not so simple to be Saint Nicholas!"

"Not by any means! Just once I wanted to give your business a try. But the beard was scratchy, and made me sneeze. And my little nephew cried out right away, 'Cheers, Uncle Erich!'"

"There you have it!" said my visitor and nodded, pleased. It seemed he was gradually warming up to me. He puffed out marvelous big smoke rings. Pola looked at him curiously. Then she sprung through one of the blue-gray rings as through a hoop, and made her way to her favorite spot, the chair under the old wall clock, to take a nap enchanted by its ticking.

"Since we're already discussing your work," I said, "I have a question for you that has preoccupied me since I was a child. I wouldn't have dared at that time. Today it is easier. As I've become a journalist in the meantime."

"Alright, then," he said, and poured himself more coffee. "What have you wanted to ask me since you were a child?"

"Well," I began hesitantly, "your job is in a sense a mobile seasonal trade, right? In December you have plenty of work. It's all compressed into a couple of weeks. You could call it a 'short-term industry.' And now…"

"Hm?"

"And now what I'd burningly like to know is what you do for the rest of the year!"

Good old Nicholas looked at me with a fairly puzzled expression. It almost gave me the impression that no one had ever asked him such an obvious question before.

"If you'd rather not reveal anything about it…"

"No, no," he grumbled. "Why not?" He gulped down some coffee and puffed out a smoke ring. "There's more than enough to do in November of course, with all the work collecting materials. In some regions there will suddenly be no chocolate. No one knows why. Or the farmers will hold back their apples. And then the drama with customs control at the border. And all the traveling papers. If things go on like this, I'll have to use up October for it too. Until now, I've really just spent October sequestering myself and letting my beard grow."

"You only wear your beard in winter?"

"Of course. I can't exactly run around all year as Santa Claus. Do you think I keep my fur coat on too? And drag that sack and switch three hundred and sixty-five days a year all over the place? Well then. —In January I draw up the balance. Horrible. Christmas gets more and more expensive, century after century!"

"I understand."

"Then I read the December mail. Before anything else, the children's letters. That holds things up colossally, but it's necessary. Otherwise you lose contact with your clientele."

"Sure."

"At the beginning of February I lose the beard."

At this moment the bell rang at the front door again. "Please excuse me." He nodded.

Outside on the landing stood a door-to-door peddler selling obnoxiously colorful picture postcards, who told me a very long and very sad tale, the first part of which I listened to bravely and with ears clenched tight.

Then I gave him the loose change I had on me, and we wished each other well. Although I refused steadfastly, he forced half a dozen of the horrid cards on me as a thank-you gift. He was, in the end, not a beggar, he said. I respected his considerable pride and relented. Finally he went away.

When I returned to the living room, I found Saint Nicholas groaning and putting his right boot back on. "I'll have to be on," he said, "it doesn't help a thing staying here. What have you got there?"

"Postcards. A peddler forced them on me. I find them rather atrocious."

"Give them here. I know a buyer. Many thanks for your warmhearted hospitality. If I wasn't Santa Claus, I might envy you."

We went to the hall, where he picked up his tools.

"Shame," I said. "You still haven't told me how you spend the rest of the year."

He shrugged his shoulders. "In truth there's not much to tell. In February I take care of the children's carnival before Lent. Later on I wander over to the spring markets. With balloons, Turkish honey, and cheap mechanical toys. I'm a lifeguard in summer and give swimming lessons. Sometimes I also sell ice-cream cones on the street. Yes, and then fall comes again, and now I really must go." We shook hands.

I watched him through the window. He trudged through the snow with big hasty strides. At the corner of Ungerer Street a man was waiting for him. He looked like the peddler, that talker with his stupid picture postcards. They went around the corner together. Or had my eyes deceived me?

⁂

Fifteen minutes later the doorbell rang once again. This time it was the errand boy from the deli, Zimmerman and Sons. A welcome visitor! He brought the grilled roast chicken that I had ordered, a small tender rolled ham, and two bottles of Piesporter Goldtröpfchen, a late vintage.

I reached to pay, but my wallet was not there.

"There's no rush, *Herr Doktor*," said the messenger paternally.

"I'd bet it's just on my desk!" I said. "But fine, I'll settle up tomorrow. Wait a moment, I'll bring you a fine cigar!"

But the box with the cigars was missing too.

Nor could I find them later. No cigars. No wallet. The silver cigarette case, likewise, was nowhere to be found. And the cuff links with the moonstones and the evening pearls were neither in their place nor anywhere else. In any case not in my apartment. I couldn't figure out where any of them might be. I certainly didn't rush to check up on my railroad stock certificates or stamp collection.

Nevertheless, it turned into a quiet, pleasant evening. The roast chicken and the Piesporter were first-class. No one else rang at the door. Behind the window snowflakes drifted down like an endless white mesh curtain. Pola woke up briefly and made woolen goulash out of a scarf. Truly a fine evening. Only something was missing. But what?

A cigar! Of course!

Luckily, my golden lighter was also nowhere to be found. For even I would admit—although I'm not easily perturbed—that to have a lighter, but nothing to smoke, could completely spoil the entire evening!

1949

THE SEPARATION

Ilse Frapan

"We fell out, my wife and I."

Dr. Beckbissinger had been separated from his wife. Everyone knew about it.

The wrong was on his side; such, the men's verdict. She was entirely to blame; so spoke the women. We may therefore take it that no one knew much either way regarding the true merits of the case. The fact of the separation, however, lay beyond dispute.

He had remained in Hamburg on account of his practice. On account of her art—she was a sculptress—she had returned to South Germany, their common home.

The affair had aged Dr. Beckbissinger by at least ten years. That, too, was well established.

People thought it came of his having never unbosomed himself to anyone, and by palpable maneuvers they tried to induce a reopening of the wound. That it must thereby find relief and heal they made no doubt. But the patient stubbornly resisted this mode of treatment, and little by little their prying concern for his heart's cure died out.

The interesting melancholy of his face furnished a fruitful topic of conversation; his slightly grizzled beard was held to contrast delightfully with the black eyebrows; and never surely did man boast so skillful or so finely shaped a hand. There would have been depths of satisfaction in discovering whether he was likely to think of a second marriage. But, alas! this proved impracticable; and as the doctor ignored the questioning glances that were directed at him, and as languishing eyes failed wholly of their purpose, he gradually sank to the level which formed, it would seem, his sole ambition, and grew to be regarded as an excellent doctor and nothing more deservedly so regarded.

This estimate of him, and his own individual leaning, brought about that he became almost exclusively a children's doctor, achieving notable success in that fruitful field of labor. He was "Uncle" to more than a hundred children, and with the little nephews and nieces of his affinity, showed himself just as talkative and merry as with their elders he was taciturn and unresponsive. Gratitude he thus earned in goodly measure, but he won few friends, unless his big tawny comrade, the St. Bernard dog, Leo, be excepted. A strange atmosphere of isolation hung about the man and his dog; unobservant people even hardly failed to be conscious of it.

"He has such an anxious mind," said Frau Sturken, his old housekeeper. "From the very first he was set on being a doctor. And all his troubles come to him along of his doctoring, for to be sure the womenfolk ran after him no end, and that was more than she could stand. It were natural enough, to my thinking, her feeling as she did ; it's but human nature for folks to want to stick to their own and not see it took away by others, and all the more when it's a matter of a doctor as must be forever on the move like any cab horse. Neither am I for blaming them other folks, for he's that sort of man well, if I'd but knowed him in time—Ah, what am I talking about! You needn't be staring at me like that. Why, I'm seventy-six, and my doctor there he'll be seven-and- forty. That wouldn't exactly fit; we're a sight too far apart. See yonder, there he goes down Bush Street, him as has the big Inverness and the big dog and the gray hat. Don't he look the gentleman?"

The object of her laudation stood talking to the postman, on whom Christmas burdens weighed heavily, and who, in addition to his bag, now carried an armful of seasonable sendings.

"Ay, doctor, there's one for you today. Half a minute while I look. Right, ain't it?" And he placed a large envelope in the doctor's hand. "Compliments of the season to you, sir."

"From Holland!" exclaimed the doctor, taken by surprise, and opening the letter as he walked along. His brow cleared at sight of a smiling face that greeted him from within the folds of the letter. The envelope contained the portrait of a little boy of about three years old. With his tiny Christmas tree upon his arm, he looked as roguish, as merry, as jolly as a plump little Santa Claus. And when in pleased astonishment the doctor had uncovered the small effigy, the best part was still to come. At the foot of the mount in the funniest of scrawls stood the words, "A merry Christmas to the preserver of my life." It was meant to look as if the three-year-old baby fingers themselves had traced the characters. What a quaint idea!

Then uprose before the doctor's inward eye a vision of those dainty little fingers tightening themselves around his own in a deadly spasm, and once more he seemed to gaze into the agonized, despairing face of the young Dutch lady, the child's mother, as she besought him not to tear the rigid hands forcibly away, and not to desert her and her dying treasure that stormy night in lonely Heligoland. And there came back to him every incident of the night and the half day following, spent mainly in a crouched position at the bedside, until the child's fingers suddenly relaxed, and sleep brought healing. He remembered having to take his food in that attitude, to eat whatever the sick child's mother thrust into his mouth. He could not help smiling at the recollection of it. To neither of them had the comic aspect of the situation then occurred; he had shared the grave anxiety of the moment; it was as if he were watching his own child's deathbed for the second time. In this picture a presentment of perfect health he was more than ever struck by a likeness between the two children, which during the boy's illness had impressed him so painfully. *A merry Christmas!* The wish was well intended, but he had done with seasons of rejoicing. *To the preserver of my life!* A sweet sound, and possibly no mere idle form of words. But ah! his own child he had not found means to save; his only child, and he had lost him. And then the tormenting reflection that everything might have turned out differently if the boy had lived! Thus even from this chance wayside blossom, meant to give only pleasure, he pressed out a bitter drop. Sighing he thrust the picture into his breast pocket.

Two men of his acquaintance came by.

"The doctor begins to age," remarked the one, "seems in the dumps today. It's a pity, such a good chap as he is."

The speaker drew himself up erect, with a consciousness of his own exemption from other men's disabilities, and both lifted their hats airily.

"Here child, Angela," said one of them, "run across to Uncle, and ask him if he will join our Christmas party tonight." Then, turning to his companion, "We live under one roof, you know. Liberty don't seem to agree with him over well, 'pon my soul. Could scarcely believe it when the thing happened. An affair of jealousy, wasn't it? Should never have credited the old boy with that sort of feeling." And he stroked his smooth banking house face complacently and winked with his small pig's eyes at the doctor across the road. "Ah, he won't, won't he? Too busy? Well, we must console ourselves. Maybe he prefers to spend the evening with countryfolk of his own."

The doctor's tall, spare form threaded its way slowly through the throng of Christmas buyers in the goose market, his gray hat seeming to float upon the human stream. Then he turned into the Dammthor Street, of which one end, stretching from the ramparts as far as the Botanical Gardens, had been converted into a veritable fir-tree plantation. The Christmas tree dealers have a fixed place here. It was a sight to see. The biggest trees were built up on each side of the pavement, and behind, extending as far as the town moat, stood innumerable others of smaller growth. The yellow gravel walk crackled with light frost; a scent of pinewoods filled the crisp air. Saleswomen with their hands thrust under their blue aprons tramped up and down to warm their feet. The space behind served as a workshop where men were now busy hacking and sawing and drilling holes. Trees do not always grow as shapely as they appear to the beholder on Christmas Eve. But the salesman's motto is, "Fraternity and Equality!" He lops a few branches off the body of an overgrown little trunk, and grafts them upon that of an ill-favored comrade: "Share and share alike!" A great heap of twigs these are in request for purposes of household decoration lay strewn around the charcoal fire at which from time to time men and women would come to warm their frost-nipped, resin-stained hands. The doctor stood still and watched. "Anything for you, sir?" asked a stout market woman, pushing her way up to him. Business was naturally brisk this evening, small trees especially being in great demand. But a big, splendid one had just then been disposed of. The buyer, a young and handsomely dressed girl, caught hold of it with her own hands; it overtopped her by a good length.

"The boy will carry it for you, miss," said the woman, pointing to him; "he'll be glad to earn a trifle."

"The boy? Well, he may carry my muff," cried the girl, and tossed it over like a ball, "but as for the tree, I must have that myself. Heavy? What matter? It's such fun to carry it."

And she shouldered it triumphantly and marched off, the boy at her heels, his hands stuck in the soft silk lining of the muff, and trying with a grin on his face to copy her tripping gait. Bystanders laughed, the doctor with them. Then a longing to buy something overcame him too. The aroma of childhood had been conjured up by those prickly shrubs; his soul became filled with an indefinable longing. His mind travelled back to the Swabian gingerbread and the tasty homemade cake that, as a lad, he had many a time been privileged to help knead into shape. Then he bethought him of the fir tree, fetched from the far depths of the forest for his sweetheart; the ranger had let him fell it with his own hands. Beneath that selfsame tree they had plighted their mutual troth. They were sitting under it, too, when suddenly a gay shower of golden nuts and apples and sugar dainties fell down about their heads. For he had chosen a pitch pine instead of a fir tree, and the heat of the room had caused its branches to droop. But they had somehow contrived to read only a glad meaning in this omen. And twice after that had they decked a tree for their boy, marking two happy years. Then the child had died, and his wife had left his house for ever, and henceforth no trees would bear their greenery for him. Yes, the people were right. His life was futile; even in his toil-filled hours he was still consumed by a burning unhealed wound.

He was moving on.

CA. 1890

EVERY YEAR ONCE AGAIN— THE CLIENT GIFT

Martin Suter

JANUARY

"Dear Dr. Keller; I'm pleased to return your good wishes and send heartfelt thanks for the lovely calendar 'Toggenburg in Seasonal Splendor,' which we received as always with great joy. Warm regards, yours, P. Probst."

Keller is puzzled. "Toggenburg in Seasonal Splendor?" But this year was "Railway Bridges of Switzerland"? Or was that last year? No, last year was "A Bird's-Eye View of Mountain Passes," to which "Railway Bridges of Switzerland" was a natural follow-up. He phones Mrs. Trösch. "'Toggenburg in Seasonal Splendor,' does that mean anything to you?"

"I often visited Toggenburg as a child," answers Mrs. Trösch, somewhat perplexed.

"We didn't send out a calendar with that name this year?"

"No, it was called 'Railway Bridges of Switzerland.'"

"I know, I know," grumbles Dr. Keller and hangs up. Then there must have been some mix-up, since Probst is hardly sarcastic. There's always the possibility that he received another calendar from someone else.

Keller has never claimed that the calendar idea was particularly original. It is more the choice of subjects and their thematic coherence that have been a source of some pride to him until now. "Toggenburg in Seasonal Splendor" seems to him rather arbitrary though. Nevertheless, if someone as meticulous as Peter Probst could mix up the calendar with "Railway Bridges of Switzerland"… Perhaps he ought from time to time to reconsider his conception of the client gift. No, it's hardly sacrosanct.

FEBRUARY

Over the course of the last year Dr. Keller has had to make many decisions, which now, as he looks back over it all, continue to preoccupy him. But that in favor of "Railway Bridges of Switzerland" is not one of them. Only once, as he looks over the balance sheets and comes across the line for "Client Gifts," does he pause for a moment out of a subconscious response to vague loose ends.

And later on once more, while traveling over a bridge on the Rhaetian Railway en route to his ski vacation, he thinks Railway Bridges? That was a good one.

MARCH

Dr. Keller returns from his ski vacation with a tan. It lends him a certain dynamic air, he thinks, that calls for corresponding action. In search of problems that one might approach with more force than deliberation, he returns to the issue of the client gift. Of course it would be a bit forcibly proactive to have this problem resolved as early as March. But he could deal with it once and for all.

Thus Dr. Keller suppresses the issue of the "calendar concept" at first. So that no one will think, "does he really have no other concerns?" he buries it offhandedly in a memo entitled "Outdated Customs," in order to ease up some gridlock, and to gather the courage to put into question some supposedly tried-and-true practices. The "calendar concept" is only one of a number of examples, along with, e.g., "overtime compensation," "office retreat," and "inflation offset."

APRIL

His mountain tan has faded, and as his complexion blanches, so daily business returns to its habitual dullness. Dr. Keller has to manage a tight budget. Whatever doesn't need to be done today has no priority. And long-term projects like the Christmas client gift are a complete extravagance. Something that a man in the position of a role model like Dr. Keller can by no means allow himself these days.

But Stefan Buser, who represents a publisher of (among other things) calendars, keeps himself from being forgotten by offering Mrs. Trösch a handsome booklet of twenty-five strawberry recipes.

MAY

As Dr. Keller spends precious time waiting for a taxi, his gaze happens to fall upon the new month's picture in "Railway Bridges of Switzerland," which hangs on the wall behind Mrs. Bucher at the reception desk. It displays an elegant viaduct in the Schinschlucht ravine. A pioneering achievement. The leitmotif that runs through all the calendars that the firm sends at year's end to its current (and prospective) clients. That was the sense to be taken from "A Bird's-Eye View of Mountain Passes" and "Hydroelectricity," a collection of twelve spectacular images of dams, always in the appropriate seasonal context. Seen in this light, Dr. Keller's concept for the client gifts is actually quite original, since it is not simply to send out calendars, but moreover to offer varied interpretations of "pioneering ideas," a concept to which the company has committed itself from day one. "Railway Bridges of Switzerland" accords with this philosophy; it is programmatic without neglecting aesthetics. It sets a high bar, thinks Dr. Keller. It won't be easy to find something on par with it. In the taxi he makes a note for himself. "Client gifts?"

JUNE

Imboden is back from his vacation to Scotland. He takes over the management meeting with the suggestion of smoked salmon. A meaningful Christmas gift, directly from the Scottish smokehouse. Imboden offers a small sampling, lays out the costs (shipping and handling from the smokehouse, gradations in weight based on the importance of each client to the company, personalized holiday greeting).

The idea isn't bad. If only it hadn't come from Imboden. But scathing rejections are offered one by one: "Isn't it a little early for salmon?" (Rüetschi). "And a little early for Christmas?" (Hess). "Wasn't there some news about worms in salmon? Or antibiotics or something?" (Baumann). "Salmon are known as the pigs of the sea." (Gruber).

Dr. Keller, who will not, even regarding client gifts, relinquish innovations to Imboden, alludes to a conceptual weakness: "It's not compelling, that's what concerns me."

"It completely implies 'pioneering ideas,'" Imboden fights back. "The elements (wind, water, fishing), innovation (direct shipping from the catch), and bilateral relations (Switzerland–Scotland)."

"Nothing against Scotland, but what's always fascinated me most about Dr. Keller's calendar idea is the Swiss connection to 'pioneering ideas,'" Rüetschi throws in.

This remark prompts Baumann to speak up again for tactical career reasons. "On the other hand, it couldn't hurt to signal a sense of openness in the client gift policy."

After a short discussion all are united against smoked salmon, but without prejudice in connection to a possible international solution. Dr. Keller determines never to allow the question of the client gift to slip out of his control. Client gifts are the tasks of bosses.

JULY

On vacation in Provence with a couple from Uster, who have been renting the house diagonally under him for years, Rüetschi meets an artist from Lausanne, who specializes in provincial landscapes depicting things as they actually look. The encounter has no immediate consequences, but should be remembered in retrospect as the developments of October/November become clear.

Baumann, who, on the way to Rimini with his family, makes a stop at a Tuscan estate that he remembers fondly from a leadership seminar, comes upon the idea of *Vino da Tavola* with individually designed labels, a service that the Swiss owner of the estate (pioneering ideas, international openness, plus Switzerland!) offers. Tasteful labels, surprisingly affordable and moreover shipped directly from the vineyard. For the rest of the trip he considers various notes for the tags and is finally satisfied with *"Buon anno!"* He enjoys the double meaning (both Happy New Year and have a good year). From time to time you must leave your troubles behind to approach things creatively.

AUGUST

A group of merry men in slightly unfashionable bathing suits wave from the banks of the Saane to the highspeed train as it whistles past across a vertiginously high bridge. A lovely image, thinks Dr. Keller as he greets Mrs. Bucher at reception on his first day back from his summer vacation. Along with "pioneering ideas" it presents the whole symbolism of different languages within Switzerland. The wholly unproblematic triumph over internal divisions.

He often thought about the client gift on vacation. And with this concrete result: he has decided to form a committee. That way the initiative remains his own, even as he delegates the work. He has also thought over the members: Imboden, because he already sought to take the task upon himself in June; Rüetschi, because of his comment during the last discussion of the issue that gave the impression, at least in this case, that he agreed conceptually with Dr. Keller; and Baumann, out of considerations of competitive strategy.

At the close of the first management meeting after the vacation, under "Miscellaneous," the committee is formed and sets a deadline: mid-October.

As he walks past Rüetschi's door a little later, he hears him say twice, loud and clear, "fucking gift." Dr. Keller smiles, but makes a note as well.

SEPTEMBER

Baumann has the natural advantage with his "Buon anno!" He can arrive to the first meeting totally relaxed and listen to what the others have to offer. He'll keep "Buon anno!" up his sleeves for the opportune moment.

Imboden's position isn't bad, either.

He has a Swiss variation of smoked salmon in mind: gravlax from a Swiss farm. Pioneering ideas, innovation, internationality, and nevertheless a national connection. The one drawback is the price. It is well over that of its imported Scottish variation. But what can be done given such strict Swiss guidelines?

Only Rüetschi's contribution remains up in the air, and he is forced to consult with his wife the night before the meeting. Something that he does only in emergencies regarding work problems, because he has the impression that it undermines his authority in this domain as well. But this time he's glad to have included her, since she rapidly, remarkably rapidly, brings the name Pierre into the mix.

"Pierre?" Rüetschi asks.

"Pierre Dubuis, the artist. The one at Bischoff's in Provence. The joker. With the landscapes."

"The drunk?" Rüetschi recalls the artist from Lausanne with the provincial landscapes. Maybe he can paint pioneering ideas on commission as well.

The first meeting of the client gift committee was held at the end of September and adjourned until the beginning of October.

OCTOBER

When Rüetschi enters the meeting room and finds it empty, he turns around. He doesn't want to be the first in for tactical reasons. After a calculated delay Imboden turns up in the meeting room, looks angrily at the clock when he finds it empty, and turns around. At the door he meets Rüetschi. "On your way to the meeting, too?" the latter asks.

"Which meeting?" Imboden responds.

The meeting room is empty when they finally go in together. They've barely sat down when the main office rings. Mr. Baumann has called from his car. He's on his way.

Until Baumann's arrival they take care to avoid the issue of the client gift. Neither thinks it wise to prematurely show his hand. But while they sit there and wait, the determination of each grows firmer to shoot down Baumann's suggestion, no matter what it is, and however inspired it may be.

They do it, too. Successfully, but at a great cost. There's not a shred left of Baumann's "Buon anno!" at the end of the first client gift meeting. But gravlax from a Swiss farm is wiped out, too. And "Tradition/Vision," a limited series of signed twelve-color prints by Pierre Dubuis, is on its last legs. They compare their calendars, set a new meeting date, and make an orderly withdrawal.

Stefan Buser, the publisher's representative, is on his way to Mrs. Trösch, to tentatively show her the calendar "Between the Sky and Earth," cable cars of Switzerland, a theme that in his opinion adheres quite nicely to his client's pioneer concept. As he passes a half-open door in the hallway of the management floor, he hears someone saying "fucking Christmas client gifts" three times, loud and clear.

NOVEMBER

"So where do we actually stand regarding the client gifts?" Dr. Keller asks at an already contentious management meeting. Imboden, Baumann, and Rüetschi exchange reproachful glances.

"Things are coming along," Rüetschi says.

"Any plans to loop me in?" Dr. Keller pointedly asks.

Rüetschi seizes the opportunity. "We're thinking about something very interesting at the moment. Pierre Dubuis. 'Tradition/Vision.' A limited series, signed. Art. Something a little different this time."

Imboden totally loses it. "I thought that was off the table. Like 'Buon anno!'"

"Or gravlax from a Swiss farm," Baumann adds, to round things out.

"It's November, gentlemen. November!" interjects Dr. Keller. In the silence that follows, Baumann lets a sentence drop that proves him to be the better tactician indeed. And the true contender to succeed Dr. Keller: "Why must we subject ourselves to this gift-giving nightmare every year?"

"What do you suggest?" Dr. Keller snaps back.

Baumann leans back. "We take the money that the gift would cost, transfer it to a charitable organization, and write a letter to our clients that explains that we regard this as the more sensible way forward in today's times. Do good and talk about it."

"Not exactly original, either," remarks Rüetschi, and gazes hopefully at Dr. Keller.

But he is considering it; a dangerous reaction. When Dr. Keller considers for any length of time an idea that did not originate with him, then it is only in order to tack something onto it, to make it suitable, and to make it his own. "How much did we aim to spend?" he finally asks.

"Thirty thousand," answers Imboden.

"Then we transfer fifteen thousand to the Red Cross. But we don't need to state the amount in the letter."

Rüetschi attempts one last time to make up some ground. "Nothing against social engagement, but are we underestimating here the fundamental purpose of Dr. Keller's calendar idea? Our year-round presence, impossible to overlook, among our clients?"

Baumann immediately notes how dangerous the objection is, and reacts with noteworthy elegance: "We can always include a calendar. Only it need not be as luxurious as in the past. On the contrary, it suits the giving spirit more if it appears more low-cost."

Dr. Keller considers. "Fifteen thousand francs, calendar and shipping included. If we find an adequate one, that should leave enough for the Red Cross. If necessary we forgo the message of pioneering ideas. Baumann, you take care of it."

Baumann maintains the dignity of a good victor for the rest of the meeting. Straight after, he goes to Mrs. Trösch, who puts him in touch with one Stefan Buser, a dependable calendar salesman.

When Buser realizes that "Between the Sky and Earth," cable cars of Switzerland, won't work for these clients for conceptual reasons, he sells Baumann a calendar for which he can offer him a good deal since it's been selling well for the third season running.

DECEMBER

In the last week before Christmas the current (and prospective) clients receive a personally signed letter from Dr. Keller that explains that in lieu of an elaborate Christmas gift, they have thought it better to make a considerable donation to the Red Cross.

The envelope contains a calendar: "Toggenburg in Seasonal Splendor."

1995

THE CHRISTMAS BOX

Johann Wolfgang von Goethe

This box, mine own sweet darling, thou wilt find
With many a varied sweetmeat's form supplied;
The fruits are they of holy Christmas tide,
But baked indeed, for children's use design'd.
I'd fain, in speeches sweet with skill combin'd,
Poetic sweetmeats for the feast provide;
But why in such frivolities confide?
Perish the thought, with flattery to blind!
One sweet thing there is still, that from within,
Within us speaks,—that may be felt afar;
This may be wafted o'er to thee alone.
If thou a recollection fond canst win,
As if with pleasure gleam'd each well-known star,
The smallest gift thou never wilt disown.

1807

IN THE OUTER SUBURBS

Peter Stamm

I'd spent Christmas Eve with friends. They'd uncorked some champagne in the afternoon, and I'd gone home early because I was drunk and I had a headache. I was living in a small studio apartment in West Queens. In the morning I was awakened by the phone. It was my parents calling from Switzerland, to wish me a merry Christmas. It wasn't a long conversation, we didn't know what else to say to each other. It was raining outside. I made myself some coffee, and read.

In the afternoon I went for a walk. For the first time since I'd been there, I headed out of town, toward the outer suburbs. I hit Queens Boulevard, and followed it east. It was a wide straight road, cutting through precincts that didn't change much or at all. Sometimes it was shops, and I had a sense of being in some sort of conurbation, and then I found myself in residential districts of tenements or small, squalid row houses. I crossed a bridge over an old, overgrown set of rails. Then there was an enclosed patch of waste ground, full of trash and rubble, and an enormous crossroads with no lights and no traffic. After that I came to another bunch of shops and a cross-street that had a subway stop on top of it, like a roof. The Christmas decorations in the storefronts and the tinsel hanging over the streets, disarrayed by rain and wind, looked like ancient remnants.

The rain had let up, and I stopped on the corner to light a cigarette. I wasn't sure whether to go on or not. Then a young woman came up to me, and asked for a light. She said it was her birthday. If I had twenty dollars on me, we could buy a few things and have ourselves a little party.

"I'm sorry," I said, "I haven't got it on me."

She said that didn't matter, I was to wait here for her anyway. She was going shopping, and would be back.

"Funny, it being your birthday on Christmas Day."

"Yes," she said, as though it had never occurred to her, "I suppose you're right."

She went off down the street, and I knew she wouldn't be back. I knew it wasn't her birthday either, but I would still have gone with her if I'd had the money. I finished my cigarette, and lit another. Then I started back. There was a bar across the street. I went in and asked for a beer.

"Are you French?" asked the man next to me. "I'm Dylan." As in the great poet Dylan Thomas, he said, *light breaks where no sun shines …*

"Did you ever," Dylan asked me, "read a love poem from a woman to a man?"

"No," I said, "I don't read poetry."

"I tell you, you're making a mistake there. You'll find everything in poetry. Everything."

He got up and went down a short flight of stairs to the restroom. When he came back, he stood next to me, put his arm around me, and said: "There aren't any! Women don't love men, believe me."

The barman gave me a signal I didn't understand. Dylan pulled a tattered volume from his pocket and held it over our heads.

"*Immortal Poems of the English Language,*" he said. "It's my bible."

There were dirty little scraps of paper stuck in between many of the pages. Dylan opened the book at a certain place.

"Now, listen to the way women love men," he said, and he read out: "Mrs. Elizabeth Barrett Browning: How do I love thee? Let me count the ways … Not one word about him. All Mrs. Browning does is say how much she loves him, how magnificent her feelings for him are. Here's another one …"

An old man next to me whispered: "He's always doing that." And he made the same signal as the barman before him. I started to get it, but I was already feeling a bit drunk, and I didn't want to go just yet. I just smiled, and turned to face Dylan who had turned to another poem.

"Miss Brontë," he said, "same story! Cold in the earth, and the deep snow piled above thee! Far, far removed ... That's how it starts, and then it's all about her pain. Nothing about the guy. Or this ... Mrs. Rossetti: My heart is like a singing bird ... My heart is like an apple tree ... And so on, till the last line, which goes: Because my love is come to me. Do you call that love? Is that the way a person in love would write? Only someone in love with herself."

He put the book away, and put his short arm around me again.

"You know, my friend, there's no such thing as a woman's love. They love us like children, or the way the creator might love the thing he's created. But as little as we find peace with God do we find peace with women."

"Does that make God a woman?" I asked.

"Of course," said Dylan, "and Jesus is Her daughter."

"And you're his sister," said the barman.

"I don't like women with beards," said the old fellow on the other side of me.

We fell silent.

"Homosexuals will all go to Hell," said the old man.

"I'm not going to get involved on that level," said Dylan angrily, and moved closer to me, as if seeking protection. "The two of us were talking about poetry. This young man here doesn't have the prejudices of you two clowns."

"The next round's on the house," said the barman, and he put a cassette of Christmas tunes on the stereo behind him.

"God rest ye, merry gentlemen," sang Harry Belafonte.

"Yo," went a young man at one of the tables, "he misadeh misadeeho ..."

The barman set our beers down on the bar in front of us. I was pretty drunk by now. I raised my glass, and said: "To poetry!"

"Well, don't say I didn't warn you," said the old man.

"Now read the poems that men have written for women," said Dylan, and he recited from memory: "She is as in a field a silken tent, at midday when a sunny summer breeze has dried the dew …"

Overcome, he stopped, looked down at the dirty floor, and sadly shook his head.

"Women call themselves romantics, as if they would call themselves American, " he said. "They love it when you say you're beautiful, your eyes shine like the sun, your lips are red as coral, your breasts are white as snow. They think they're romantic because they like to be adored by men."

I wanted to contradict, but he said: "I just want to open your eyes. Don't let women make a fool of you. They'll tempt you with their spare flesh. And once you've bitten, they'll break your head open and eat you up."

I laughed.

"You remind me of someone," said Dylan.

"Some friend of yours?" I asked.

"A very good friend. He's dead now."

I went to the restroom.

"I've got no money left for the bus now," I said.

"I'll take you home," said Dylan.

I thought it must be dark by now, but as we stepped out of the bar, it was a fine afternoon. The rain had stopped.

There were still clouds in the sky. But the low sun shone through underneath them. The houses and trees and cars glistened and projected long shadows. Dylan had his car parked on Queens Boulevard. He turned into a side street.

"That's not my way home," I said. "You're going the wrong way."

Dylan laughed. "Are you scared of me?" he asked.

I didn't say anything.

"I'm just turning the car around," he said. "Are you that scared of women too?"

"I don't know … I guess not."

We drove back toward Manhattan in silence. I hadn't walked nearly as far as I thought.

"Here," I said, "I'd like to walk the last bit."

I got out, and walked around the car. Dylan had wound down the window and held out his hand.

"Thanks for the ride," I said, "and thanks for the beer."

Dylan wouldn't let go my hand till I looked into his eyes. Then he said: "Thanks for a pleasant afternoon."

As I crossed the street, he called after me: "And Merry Christmas."

1999

ADVENT

Rainer Maria Rilke

A wind through woods in winter driving
the herds of snowflakes like a flock,
and certain firs foresee they'll shortly
be donning sanctifying light;
and listen close. The pale white pathways
stretching the branches forth—prepared,
and against the gusts and growing into
the single night of glory praised.

1898

CHRISTMAS SHOPPING

Arthur Schnitzler

Light snow is falling at six o'clock on Christmas Eve. Anatol, *a pleasure-seeking Viennese, is rushing along a street lined with shops, and catches up to* Gabrielle, *one of his former lovers.*

Anatol [stopping]—Dear lady, dear lady … !

Gabrielle—I beg your pardon … Oh, it's you!

Anatol—Yes, I've been running after you! I can't just watch while you carry all these things. Let me take some of your packages … Please.

Gabrielle—No, no, thank you—I'll carry them myself!

Anatol—But I beg you, allow me some gallantry for once.

Gabrielle—Well, you could take just this one.

Anatol—That's nothing. Let me take this one, and this … and the other.

Gabrielle—Enough, that's enough—you're too kind!

Anatol—It does one good when one can be.

Gabrielle—You only seem to give evidence of that when you're out in public—and it's snowing.

Anatol—And when it's getting late into the evening, and when it just happens to be Christmas?

Gabrielle—It's astounding that you happen to show up!

Anatol—Yes, yes … You mean that I haven't visited you even once this year.

Gabrielle—Yes, something like that.

Anatol—I haven't been visiting anyone this year—no one at all! So, how's your fine husband doing? And the dear children?

Gabrielle—Please spare me such questions—I know none of that is really of interest to you.

Anatol—It's uncanny how well you can read me!

Gabrielle—Well, I do know you!

Anatol—Not as well as I might wish!

Gabrielle—Stop it with such comments! Yes…

Anatol—Oh, I can't help myself.

Gabrielle—Then give me back my packages!

Anatol—Don't get angry, I'll behave myself …

[*They walk along together in silence.*]

Gabrielle—You could at least say something!

Anatol—Something—for sure—but you're so critical…

Gabrielle—Do tell me something. We haven't seen each other for such a long time… What have you been doing?

Anatol—I haven't been doing anything, as usual!

Gabrielle—Nothing?

Anatol—Nothing at all!

Gabrielle—That's really a shame!

Anatol—You really don't care in any case!

Gabrielle—How can you say that?

Anatol—Why do I waste my life? Who's to blame for that? Who?

Gabrielle—Give me my packages!

Anatol—I don't accuse anyone… I'm just asking.

Gabrielle—You still spend your time strolling around idly?

Anatol—Idly! You put it so contemptuously! As if there were anything better than idling! But that's certainly not the case this evening. I'm just as busy as you are, dear lady!

Gabrielle—How's that?

Anatol—I'm also going Christmas shopping!

Gabrielle—You!?

Anatol—But I really can't find anything worth buying! I've been standing for weeks every evening in front of the shop windows in all the streets. But with these merchants there's nothing tasteful or inspired to be found.

Gabrielle—Taste and inspiration are up to the customer to provide! If someone has so little to do as you, you'd be so inspired that you'd take care of all the Christmas shopping already in the fall.

Anatol—I'm not that sort. How would you know already in the fall to whom you'll give a gift? And now it's just two hours before the shops close and I have no idea, no clue!

Gabrielle—May I help you?

Anatol—You're an angel, but don't take back these packages.

Gabrielle—No, no.

Anatol—You let me call you an angel, darling angel.

Gabrielle—Oh, please stop it!

Anatol—I'll behave myself.

Gabrielle—So, give me some sense of what you might want to buy. Whom would this gift be for?

Anatol—That's a little hard to say…

Gabrielle—A lady, naturally?!

Anatol—Well, yes. As I said before, you do know me quite well.

Gabrielle—But what kind of woman—a true lady?

Anatol—It depends on what you mean by that. If you mean a woman who moves in your circles, then perhaps not.

Gabrielle—Is it someone I might know?

Anatol—I think not.

Gabrielle—Well, I certainly didn't think so!

Anatol—Don't be so snide!

Gabrielle—I know your type—someone thin and blonde, who lives outside the city center.

Anatol—She's blonde, I'll admit.

Gabrielle—Blonde, it's odd how you're always involved with these women from the outer districts.

Anatol—I'm not to blame, dear lady.

Gabrielle—Don't be unfair. It's good that you follow your taste and enjoy your conquests.

Anatol—What else should I do—I like to have my admirers.

Gabrielle—But do they really understand you?

Anatol—I have no idea! But you know… the common women merely cherish me while the grandes dames only manage to understand me.

Gabrielle—I don't know about that and I don't want to. Come along, here's just the right shop where we can buy something for your little friend.

Anatol—Oh, dear lady!

Gabrielle—Now, let's see. Look at this lovely box containing three different scents, or this one with six types of soaps—Patchouli, Bergamot, Jockey Club—those might do, no?

Anatol—Dear lady, you're being unkind!

Gabrielle—Oh, wait, here! Look, this little broach with six rhinestones—just think—six! How they sparkle! Or this charming bracelet with heavenly charms—these glittering things should appeal to someone like that!

Anatol—Dear lady, you're mistaken. You don't even know the girl, and she's quite different than you imagine.

Gabrielle—Oh, how lovely! Come closer! What do you think of that hat! That style was all the rage two years ago! And the feathers, how they flutter! That would certainly attract lots of attention!

Anatol—Dear lady, you underestimate her taste.

Gabrielle—It's not easy with you. If you want my help, you'll have to give me a little more to go on.

Anatol—How can I do that, when you'd only respond with derisive laughter?

Gabrielle—Oh, no, no! Help me to understand. Is she vain or demure, large or small? Does she favor bright colors?

Anatol—I shouldn't have taken your friendliness for granted. All you can do is mock.

Gabrielle—Not at all, I'm listening. Tell me about her.

Anatol—But I hardly dare.

Gabrielle—Oh, do. How long…?

Anatol—Let's forget about it!

Gabrielle—I insist! How long have you known her?

Anatol—For… a long time!

Gabrielle—Don't make me ask so many questions. Tell me the whole story!

Anatol—There's not much of a story.

Gabrielle—But where did you meet her, how, and when, and what kind of person is she, that's what I really want to know!

Anatol—Alright, but it's all a bit boring, I'm telling you.

Gabrielle—It truly interests me. I'd like to know something about her world. What kind of milieu is it? I can't even imagine!

Anatol—You couldn't begin to comprehend it!

Gabrielle—Oh, *mein Herr*!

Anatol—You have such overarching contempt for anyone not belonging to your circle. That's terribly unjust.

Gabrielle—But I'm eager to learn. How can I learn about this milieu if no one dares to tell me about it?

Anatol—But it seems that you have a vague feeling that she's somehow getting the better of you in the end?

Gabrielle—I beg to differ, no one takes anything away from me that I want to keep for myself.

Anatol—Yes, but when it's something that you don't really want… then it still bothers you when someone else gets it?

Gabrielle—Oh—!

Anatol—That's a woman's natural prerogative. And since it's a woman's prerogative, it's probably also refined, beautiful and deep …

Gabrielle—You've become so sarcastic!

Anatol—And how would that have come about? I'll tell you. I used to be so good and trusting and spoke without scorn, but I've suffered some blows.

Gabrielle—Don't romanticize!

Anatol—True wounds, yes. A rejection, coming from the most beloved lips, that I could survive. But a "No" when the eyes emphatically say "Perhaps," when the lips smile seductively to signal "Could be!" and when the tone of voice sounds like "Certainly," that kind of a rejection is…

Gabrielle—Let's get on with the shopping!

Anatol—Such rejections turn you into a fool … or a cynic!

Gabrielle—You wanted to tell me about it…

Anatol—Good, if you really want to hear it all.

Gabrielle—Of course, I do! How did you meet her?

Anatol—How does one meet anyone? On the street, at a dance, on the omnibus, under an umbrella…

Gabrielle—You know this special case interests me. We want to buy something special just for her.

Anatol—There are no special cases among such women, nor among those in your own circle. You're all so typical!

Gabrielle—You're starting up again…

Anatol—I don't mean to be insulting—certainly not—I'm just a type myself!

Gabrielle—And what sort are you?

Anatol—I am a Reckless Melancholic!

Gabrielle—And I am?

Anatol—You are a Worldly Married Lady!

Gabrielle—And, she is…?

Anatol—She's a sweet girl!

Gabrielle—Sweet? Right away sweet? And I—worldly—pure and simple?

Anatol—Naughtily worldly, if you really want to know.

Gabrielle—So, finally, tell me about her, the sweet girl.

Anatol—She's not incredibly beautiful, nor overly elegant, and she's not so clever…

Gabrielle—I don't want to know what she's not.

Anatol—But she has the gentle charm of a spring evening, the grace of an enchanted princess, and the spirit of a maiden who knows how to love!

Gabrielle—This kind of spirit must be quite commonplace among her kind!

Anatol—You can't begin to put yourself in her place! Too much was kept from you when you were a young girl, and you were told too much since you became a young woman! That's the origin of the naiveté of your observations.

Gabrielle—But listen to me, I'd like to understand. I believe you when you say she's an enchanted princess. Tell me about the castle in which she lives.

Anatol—You of course shouldn't imagine a glittering salon, with heavy doors, decorative objects and velvet strewn around in the staged half-light of a dying afternoon …

Gabrielle—I don't want to know what I should not imagine …

Anatol—So, picture a small gloomy room, very small with painted walls, a few mediocre etchings here and there, a hanging lamp with a shade. From the window you can see roofs and chimneys and when spring comes the garden opposite blooms and smells sweet.

Gabrielle—How happy she must be to spend Christmas already looking forward to May.

Anatol—Yes, I'm sometimes happy there myself!

Gabrielle—That's enough, enough! It's getting late and we need to buy her something. Perhaps something for her shabby room.

Anatol—It doesn't lack anything!

Gabrielle—Yes, I'm sure that she doesn't need anything, but I'd like to decorate the room a bit more to your taste!

Anatol—My taste?

Gabrielle—With Persian carpets …

Anatol—That's not necessary.

Gabrielle—Some bibelots?

Anatol—Hm!

Gabrielle—A pair of vases with fresh flowers?

Anatol—But I want to bring *her* something …

Gabrielle—Yes, yes, we need to decide. She's probably waiting for you?

Anatol—Certainly!

Gabrielle—Tell me, what does she say when she greets you?

Anatol—The usual.

Gabrielle—She recognizes your step in the stairwell?

Anatol—Yes, sometimes.

Gabrielle—And she waits for you at the door?

Anatol—Yes!

Gabrielle—And she throws her arms around your neck, kisses you, and then what does she say?

Anatol—The right things.

Gabrielle—For example?

Anton—I can't give one.

Gabrielle—So what did she say to you yesterday?

Anatol—*Ach*, nothing special … It sounds so ordinary when you can't hear the tone of her voice…

Gabrielle—I will imagine it. What does she say?

Anatol—"It's wonderful to have you back again!"

Gabrielle—"It's wonderful …" What was the rest?

Anatol—"to have you back again."

Gabrielle—That's lovely, very lovely!

Anatol—Yes, it's heartfelt and true.

Gabrielle—And she's always there alone? You can see each other without being disturbed?

Anatol—Yes, she's by herself, all alone. No father, no mother, not even an aunt.

Gabrielle—And you're her everything?

Anatol—… It's possible! … This evening … [*He goes silent.*]

Gabrielle—It's getting so late. Look how empty the streets have become …

Anatol—Oh, I'm keeping you. You need to get home.

Gabrielle—Of course, they're waiting for me. But what are we going to do about the gift?

Anatol—I'll find some trifle.

Gabrielle—But I wanted to help you find something for the sweet thing.

Anatol—It's fine.

Gabrielle—How I wish I could be there when you bring her the Christmas present… I'd love to see the small room and the sweet girl. She has no idea how lucky she is!

Anatol—Mm…

Gabrielle—But now give me my packages. It's so late!

Anatol—Here you are, but there's a cab.

Gabrielle—Could you wave it down?

Anatol—You're in a hurry, all of a sudden?!

Gabrielle—Please! [*He waves down the taxi.*] I thank you. But what are we doing to do about the gift …?

Anatol—Here, it's stopped.

Gabrielle—Here, please take these flowers, these simple flowers. They're nothing more than a greeting, but please give them to her for me.

Anatol—Dear lady—you're so kind.

Gabrielle—You promise me?

Anatol—With pleasure, why not?

Gabrielle—So tell her…

Anatol—Yes?

Gabrielle—So tell her: "These flowers, my … sweet girl, are sent to you by a woman, who can love just as well as you, but who didn't have the courage…"

Anatol—Dear … lady!?

[*She gets into the taxi, it drives off as he watches it disappear. He stands still for a moment, looks at his watch and rushes off. Curtain*]

1893

CHRISTMAS WITH THE BUDDENBROOKS

Thomas Mann

"Shout for joy, Jerusalem!" the choirboys sang to end their program, and after a kind of interwoven fugue, the voices arrived in joyful, peaceful harmony at the last syllable. The echoes of the chord faded away, and deep silence lay over the columned hall and the landscape room. Under the weight of the long pause, all the members of the family gazed at their feet. Only Hugo Weinschenk's eyes roamed, bold and unperturbed, around the room. Frau Permaneder coughed an audible dry cough that she simply could not suppress. Madame Buddenbrook, however, slowly strode to the table and joined her family, taking a seat on the sofa, which no longer stood off to itself at some distance from the table, as in the old days. She adjusted the lamp and pulled the large Bible over to her—the gilt on its immense embossed cover faded with age. Then she set her glasses on her nose, undid the colossal book's two leather clasps, opened it to the bookmark, revealing a heavy, coarse, yellowed page of huge print, took a sip of sugar-water, and began to read the Christmas story.

She read the familiar old words slowly, stressing each in a clear, stirring voice, her joy rising above the pious hush—and all hearts were touched. "And on earth peace, good will toward men," she said. And no sooner did she fall silent than the columned hall was filled with harmonious voices singing "Silent night, holy night," and the family in the landscape room joined in. They went about it rather cautiously, because most of them were not musical, and now and then a deep voice would sound a note quite inappropriate to the ensemble. But that did not detract from the effect. Frau Permaneder's lips quivered as she sang, for the carol sounded sweetest and saddest to a woman whose heart had known a troubled life and who could cast an eye back over it now in this brief, peaceful, solemn hour. Madame Kethelsen wept silent, bitter tears, although she could hear almost nothing.

And now old Madame Buddenbrook stood up. She grasped the hands of her grandson, Johann, and her great-granddaughter, Elisabeth, and strode across the room. The older ladies and gentlemen closed ranks behind her, the younger ones followed and were joined in the columned hall by the servants and the "poor," and they all lifted their voices in "O, Tannenbaum"—and Uncle Christian made the children laugh by lifting his legs like a funny, marching marionette and singing the silly words "Oh, Tinny Boom." And with every eye sparkling and a smile on every face, they marched through the wide-open folding doors into heaven.

The whole room was fragrant with lightly-singed evergreen boughs and glowed and sparkled with the light of countless little flames; the sky-blue wallpaper with its white statues of gods made the large room look even brighter. Set between the dark red of the curtained windows stood the mighty Christmas tree, towering almost to the ceiling—a shining angel at the top, a sculptured manger scene at the base; it was decorated with silvery tinsel and white lilies and flooded by the soft light of the candle flames that flickered like distant stars. A row of smaller trees trimmed with candy and more burning wax candles had been arranged on the table, which extended from the window almost to the door, its whole length covered with a white linen cloth and laden with gifts. The gas jets along the walls were lit, and thick candles were burning on four candelabra, one set in each corner of the room. The larger presents that did not fit on the table had been placed in a long row on the floor. At either side of the door were smaller tables, likewise covered with white linen, each ornamented by a little tree with candles aflame and laden with presents—the gifts for the servants and the "poor."

Dazzled by the light and feeling out of place somehow in the familiar old room, they went on singing as they filed past the manger, where a waxen baby Jesus appeared to be making the sign of the cross; and then, after a quick glance at the various decorations, they took their places and fell silent.

Hanno was completely confused now. The moment he entered the room, he had spotted the theater that his eyes were seeking so feverishly—there on the table, a splendid theater, looking much larger and grander than he had even dared imagine. But Hanno had ended up in a different place, directly across from where he had stood the year before, and this so disconcerted him that he seriously doubted whether that marvelous theater was really meant for him. Something else bothered him, too—sitting on the floor, right below the stage, was a large, strange object, something that he had not asked for. A piece of furniture, a kind of wardrobe, perhaps? Was that for him?

"Come here, my child, and look at this," Madame Buddenbrook said, opening the lid. "I know how you love to play chorales. Herr Pfühl will give you whatever lessons are necessary. You have to pump with your feet the whole time, sometimes harder and sometimes not so hard. And you never lift your hands, but only change your finger positions *peu à peu.*"

It was a harmonium, a pretty little harmonium of polished brown wood with metal handles on both sides, a brightly colored treadle bellows, and a graceful little revolving stool. Hanno played a chord—and a gentle organ tone was released, so that all the others in the room looked up from their own gifts. Hanno hugged his grandmother, who pressed him gently to her; then she let him go and began to receive the thanks of everyone else.

He turned to his theater. The harmonium was like an overpowering dream, but he had no time to explore it more closely just yet. There was such a surfeit of good things that you could only pass quickly from one to the next, trying first to get some picture of the whole, but without feeling real gratitude for any single item. Oh, look, there was a prompter's box, shaped like a seashell, and behind it was the red-and-gold curtain that rolled up majestically. The stage was set for the final act of *Fidelio.* The poor prisoners stood with their hands folded; Don Pizarro, with massive puffy sleeves, stood in the foreground, striking a terrifying pose; and striding hastily in from the rear came the minister, who was dressed all in black and would now set everything to rights. It was just like in the municipal theater—almost even more beautiful. The jubilant chorus of the finale echoed in Hanno's ears, and he sat down at his harmonium, intending to play the part of it that he remembered. But then he stood up again and reached for the book of Greek mythology that he had asked for—it was bound all in red, with a golden Pallas Athena on the cover. He first sampled some candy, marzipan, and gingerbread from his plate, then inspected the smaller items—writing utensils and notebooks—and forgot everything else when he saw the penholder, topped by a tiny glass sphere. It was like magic—if you held it up to your eye, you suddenly saw a whole Swiss landscape.

Mamselle Severin and the housemaid now moved about the room with refreshments, and Hanno found time to look about him as he sat dunking a cookie in his tea. Chatting and laughing, people stood beside the table or walked up and down alongside it, showing off their own gifts or admiring those of others. There were objects of every sort—made of porcelain, nickel, silver, and gold, of wood, silk, and linen. On the table was a long row of gingerbread cakes, glazed and sprinkled with almonds, alternating with loaves of marzipan bread, so fresh they were still moist inside. The presents that Frau Permaneder had wrapped or decorated—a needlework bag, a doily to put under a potted plant, a hassock—were trimmed with large satin bows.

Now and then relatives came over to little Johann, and laying an arm on his shoulder and stroking his sailor-suit collar, they would examine his presents and admire them with the ironic exaggeration adults typically show for the treasures of children. Only Uncle Christian was free of this adult arrogance. He sauntered over to Hanno's chair—he wore a new diamond ring, a gift from his mother—and he was as delighted with the puppet theater as his nephew.

"By George, that's a dandy!" he said, raising and lowering the curtain; he took a step back to size up the scenery. He fell silent, looking strangely serious, as if troubled by something, and his eyes wandered about the room, "Did you ask for it?—I see, so you asked for this, did you?" he suddenly said. "Now, why was that? Where did you get that idea? Have you ever been to the theater?—Oh, you saw *Fidelio*, did you? Yes, they did it well. And now you want to stage it yourself, is that it? Put on your own operas? It impressed you that much, did it? Well, listen to me, boy, let me give you some advice.

Don't spend your time thinking too much about such things—theater and all that. It won't get you anywhere—trust your uncle. I've always been too interested in the stage myself, and I've never amounted to much. I've made some big mistakes, let me tell you."

He lectured his nephew with sober insistence, while Hanno looked up at him in curiosity. But then, after a pause, during which his bony, gaunt face brightened again as he examined the theater, he suddenly brought one of the figures forward on the stage and, in a hollow, croaking vibrato, began to sing, "Oh, what horrible offenses!" And then he pushed the harmonium stool over in front of the stage, sat down, and began putting on an opera, singing and gesticulating, now waving his arms in imitation of the conductor, now playing the various roles. Several members of the family gathered behind him, laughing and shaking their heads in amusement. Hanno watched with genuine delight. After a while, however, to everyone's surprise, Christian suddenly stopped. He fell silent and a restless, earnest look passed over his face; he rubbed his hand across his bald head and then down his whole left side. He turned around now to his audience—his nose wrinkled up, his face drawn and anxious.

"You see, as usual I have to stop," he said. "The same old punishment. I can never have a little fun without paying for it. It's not a pain, really, it's an ache, a vague ache, because all these nerves here are too short. They're all simply too short."

But his relatives took his complaints no more seriously than his jokes and said little or nothing in reply. They casually drifted away again. Christian sat staring mutely at the theater for a while, blinking his eyes as if deep in thought. Then he got up again.

"Well, my boy, have fun with it," he said, stroking Hanno's hair. "But not too much. And don't neglect your schoolwork because of it, do you hear? I've made my share of mistakes.... But now I'm off to the Club. I'm going to the Club for a bit," he called to the other adults. "They're having a Christmas party, too. Until later." And he left, walking down the columned hall on stiff, bowed legs.

Since they had all eaten lunch earlier than usual today, they consumed large amounts of cookies and tea. But no sooner had they finished than a large crystal bowl filled with a yellow, grainy puree was passed around: almond crème, a mixture of eggs, ground almonds, and rose water. It tasted quite wonderful, but one spoonful too much and you ended up with the most awful stomachache. Nevertheless, even though Madame Buddenbrook begged them "to leave a little corner for dinner," they helped themselves freely. And Klothilde performed miracles. In grateful silence, she spooned up almond crème as if it were porridge. And now came little glasses of sabayon to refresh their palates—served with English plum cake. Gradually they drifted back into the landscape room and, setting their plates down, gathered in little groups around the table.

Hanno stayed behind in the dining room alone. Little Elisabeth had been taken home, but for the first time he was to be allowed to stay for Christmas dinner on Meng Strasse. The servants and the "poor" had departed with their gifts, and out in the columned hall Ida Jungmann was chatting with Rieke Severin—although, as a governess, Ida as usual preserved a proper social distance when talking with a domestic. The candles on the tall tree had burned down and gone out, leaving the manger in darkness; but a few candles were still burning on the trees on the table; now and then a sprig would crackle as it was singed by a nearby flame, adding to the fragrance that filled the room. The least breath of air brushing the trees made the tinsel shudder and tinkle in metallic whispers. It was still enough again now to hear the barrel organ's soft tones floating in from a distant street on the cold night air.

Hanno surrendered himself to the scents and sounds of Christmas. His head propped in one hand, he read his mythology book and, giving the day its due, mechanically snacked on candy, marzipan, almond crème, and plum cake. The heavy uneasiness of an overfilled stomach blended with the sweet excitement of the evening to create a sense of melancholy bliss. He read about Zeus's struggles to become ruler of the gods, and now and then he would listen for a moment to the conversation in the living room, an extended discussion about Aunt Klothilde's future.

Klothilde was by far the happiest person in the house that night. She accepted their congratulations and the general teasing with a smile that turned her ash-gray face radiant. When she spoke her voice would break with sheer joy. She had been accepted by the Johannes Cloister. Working quietly behind the scenes on the board of directors, the senator had got her admitted, although certain gentlemen had muttered in private about nepotism. They were talking now about this meritorious institution, the equal of any home for aristocratic ladies in Mecklenburg, Dobbertin, or Ribnitz, which offered suitable care and a dignified old age for indigent spinsters from established families. Poor Klothilde was now assured a small but secure pension, which would increase with the passing years, and when, as an old woman, she had finally moved into the highest bracket, she would even be given a quiet, tidy apartment in the cloister.

Little Johann spent a few minutes with the adults, but soon returned to the dining room—it was not so bright now and its glories were not so bewildering and intimidating as before, lending it a whole new charm. He found a strange delight in roaming about as if this were a half-darkened stage after the curtain had fallen and he could peek behind the scenery—he took a closer look at the tall tree's lilies with their golden stamens, picked up the animal and human figurines of the crèche, located the candle that had illumined the transparent star above the stable of Bethlehem, and raised the long panel of white cloth to look at all the boxes and packing paper piled under the table.

Besides, the conversation in the landscape room was becoming less and less interesting. Gradually, ineluctably, it had turned to the one dreadful theme that had been on everyone's mind all evening, but about which they had all been silent until now, out of respect for the festivities—Herr Weinschenk's trial. Hugo Weinschenk gave a little survey of the matter, with a kind of wild cheerfulness in his expression and gestures. The trial was now in recess because of the holidays, but he reported in detail the testimony of various witnesses, was very lively in his censure of Dr. Philander, the presiding judge, whose biases were only too obvious, and with masterful scorn he criticized the mocking tone that the prosecutor, Dr. Hagenström, had thought appropriate when addressing him or witnesses in his defense. But Breslauer had very wittily weakened various pieces of incriminating evidence and had assured him in no uncertain terms that there was no reason at present even to think of a conviction. Now and then the senator would ask a polite question, and Frau Permaneder, who was sitting on the sofa with her shoulders raised high, would mutter occasionally, calling dreadful curses down on Moritz Hagen-ström. The others, however, said not a word. Their silence was so profound that Hugo Weinschenk gradually fell silent himself; and whereas in the next room time sped past for Hanno on angels' wings, a heavy, oppressive, anxious silence lay over the landscape room—and continued until Christian returned at half past eight from the Club's Christmas party for bachelors and suitors.

A cold cigar butt was wedged between his lips, and his cheeks were flushed. He entered by way of the dining room and, stepping into the land-scape room, said, "Well, children, the tree still looks gorgeous. Weinschenk, we really should have invited Breslauer to join us this evening—I'm sure he's never seen anything like it."

His mother cast him a silent, reproachful glance. But the candid, ques-tioning look on his face was one of perfect incomprehension. At nine o'clock they sat down to dinner.

As always on Christmas Eve, the table had been set in the columned hall. Madame Buddenbrook said the traditional grace with great fervor: "Come, Lord Jesus, be our guest and bless what Thou hast given us." As always on Christmas Eve, she concluded with a little admonition, the primary thrust of which was that on this holy night they should remember all those who were not as fortunate as the Buddenbrook family. And once this was taken care of, they sat down with a good conscience to a lengthy meal, which began with carp in drawn butter and a vintage Rhenish wine.

The senator slipped a few of the fish scales into his wallet so that it would not lack for money throughout the coming year, but Christian remarked gloomily that that was never any help. Consul Kröger had long since dispensed with such precautionary measures. He no longer had any reason to fear the fluctuations of the market—his ship had arrived safely in harbor, even if with only a shilling or two. The old gentleman sat as far away as possible from his wife, with whom he had spoken hardly a single word for years, because she persisted in secretly sending money to disinherited Jakob, who at present was in London, Paris, or America—only she knew for sure. They were on the second course, and the conversation had turned to absent members of the family; he scowled forbiddingly when he noticed the boy's weak-willed mother dry her eyes. They spoke of relatives in Frankfurt and Hamburg, even mentioned Pastor Tiburtius in Riga without ill will; and the senator and his sister, Tony, privately raised their glasses in a toast to Herr Grünlich and Herr Permaneder, who in some sense were still part of the family.

The turkey, stuffed with chestnuts, raisins, and apples, was praised by all. Comparisons were made with birds of years past, and it was concluded that this was the largest in a long time. There were roast potatoes, plus two kinds of vegetables and two kinds of stewed fruit, the bowls heaped so full that each looked like a hearty filling main course, rather than a side dish. They drank vintage red wine from the house of Möllendorpf.

Little Johann sat between his parents and managed to force down a piece of white meat and some dressing. He certainly could not eat as much as Aunt Thilda, and he felt tired and a little queasy. But all the same, he was proud that he was allowed to dine with the adults, proud that one of those tasty buns strewn with poppyseed had been placed on his napkin, too, and that there were three wine glasses set at his place, whereas normally he drank from the little gold beaker that Uncle Kröger had given him at his christening. But then, when Uncle Justus began pouring some oily, yellow Greek wine in the smallest glasses and the iced meringues appeared—red, white, and brown—his appetite returned. He ate a red one, although it hurt his teeth something awful, and then half of a white, and had to sample at least a little of the brown one, filled with chocolate ice cream. He nibbled on a little waffle, too, and sipped at the sweet wine while he listened to Uncle Christian, who was talking now.

He told about the Christmas party at the Club, which had been very festive. "Good God," he said in the same tone of voice he used when speaking of Johnny Thunderstorm, "those fellows were drinking brandy smash like water!"

"How awful!" Madame Buddenbrook said curtly, lowering her eyes.

But he paid no attention. His eyes began to roam, and his thoughts and memories were so vivid that they flitted like shadows across his face. "Do any of you know," he asked, "what it's like when you've drunk too much brandy smash? I don't mean being drunk, but what it's like the next day. The after-effects are curious and disgusting—yes, curious and disgusting at the same time."

"Reason enough for a precise description, I suppose," the senator said.

"*Assez*, Christian, we are not the least bit interested," Elisabeth Buddenbrook said.

But he paid no attention. One of his idiosyncrasies was that at such moments he was impervious to all objections. He was silent for a while, but then suddenly what he had to say appeared to have ripened, and he went on. "You go around feeling rotten," he said and turned a wrinkled-up nose to his brother. "Your head aches and your bowels are not in good shape—but, then, that's the case on other occasions as well. But you feel dirty"—and here Christian screwed up his face and rubbed his hands together—"you feel dirty, as if you needed a bath. You wash your hands, but that does no good, they still feel clammy and unclean, and your fingernails are oily somehow. You take a bath, but that doesn't help, your whole body feels sticky and grubby. There's something annoying about your whole body, it itches, you're disgusted with yourself. Do you know the feeling, Thomas, do you know it?"

"Yes, yes," the senator said with a dismissive wave of his hand. But with an extraordinary tactlessness that had grown only worse over the years, Christian went right on—never stopping to think that the entire explanation was embarrassing everyone at the table, that it was totally out of place in such surroundings on such an evening—and described the wretched condition that resulted from overdoing the pleasures of brandy smash, until finally he decided that he had presented it in sufficient detail and gradually lapsed into silence.

Before the last course of butter and cheese was served, old Madame Buddenbrook used the opportunity for another little speech. Even though not everything had turned out over the years quite the way one, out of shortsightedness, might have wished, she said, nevertheless there still remained such manifold and obvious blessings that their hearts should be filled with gratitude. Indeed, the interplay of moments of happiness and affliction only proved that God had never lifted His hand from the family, but that He had guided, and would continue to guide, its fortunes according to His deep and wise plan, which one ought never make bold to fathom out of impatience. And now with hopeful hearts, they ought to raise a toast in harmony to the family's health and to its future, to a future that would still continue long after its oldest members present this evening had gone to their rest in the coolness of the grave—and so, then, a toast to the children, to whom this holiday truly belonged.

And since the Weinschenks' daughter was no longer present, it was little Johann who had to make the round of the table all alone, and while they all exchanged a general toast, he had to lift his glass with each, starting with his grandmother and ending with Mamselle Severin. When he came to his father, the senator touched his glass to his son's and gently raised the boy's chin to look into his eyes. But he did not find them, because Hanno had let his long, golden-brown lashes fall deep, deep—until they covered the delicate bluish shadows beneath his eyes.

Therese Weichbrodt, however, took his head in both hands, kissed him on each cheek with a soft popping sound, and said in a voice so sincere that God Himself would have found it irresistible, "Be heppy, you good chawld!"

An hour later, Hanno lay in his bed, which had recently been placed in a little room off the third-floor corridor, just to the left of the senator's dressing room. He was lying on his back, out of deference to his stomach, which was not on good terms with all the things it had been forced to take in over the course of the evening; but he looked up with bright eyes as good old Ida, already dressed in her nightgown, entered from her room with a water glass, which she swirled in little circles as she brought it to him. He quickly drank the bicarbonate, made a face, and fell back into his bed.

"I think I'm really going to have to throw up now, Ida."

"There, there, Hanno. Just lie still on your back. But you see now, don't you? Who kept trying to warn you with little signals? And who wouldn't listen? The little boy, that's who."

"Yes, well, maybe I'll be all right after all. When will my presents arrive, Ida?"

"In the morning, my boy."

"Have them brought up here. So I can have them right away!"

"All right, Hanno, but first you have to get a good night's sleep." And she kissed him, put out the light, and left.

He was alone, and as he lay there quietly enjoying the beneficial effects of the bicarbonate, he closed his eyes and saw again the dining room full of gifts, glowing in all its brilliance. Somewhere in the distance he could hear choirboys singing "Shout for joy, Jerusalem," and he saw his theater, his harmonium, and his mythology book—the whole glittering scene. His head buzzed with a gentle fever, and under the disquieting pressure of his upset stomach, his heartbeat was slow, strong, and irregular. He lay there for a long time feeling queasy, excited, weary, anxious, and happy, and could not fall asleep.

1901

CHRISTMAS NOT JUST ONCE A YEAR

Heinrich Böll

I t is simple enough with hindsight to discern the origin of a disquieting trend—and, strangely enough, it is only now, when I observe the situation pragmatically, that the things which have been occurring in the family for almost two years seem unusual.

It might have struck us earlier that something was not right. In fact, something wasn't right, and if anything at all has ever been right—which I doubt—here things are occurring that fill me with horror. Throughout the family, Aunt Milla had always been known for her particular fondness for decorating the Christmas tree, a harmless if particular weakness that is fairly widespread in our Fatherland. Her weakness met with smiles all around, and the resistance displayed by Franz from his earliest youth to this "to-do" was always the object of vehement indignation, especially since Franz cut a disquieting figure anyway. He refused to help decorate the tree. Up to a certain point, all this took a normal course. My aunt had become accustomed to Franz's staying away from the pre-Christmas preparations, even from the actual celebration, appearing only for Christmas dinner. It was no longer even discussed.

At the risk of making myself unpopular, I must now mention a fact in defense of which I can only say that it really is one. During the years 1939 to 1945 there was a war on. In wartime there is a lot of singing, shooting, talking, fighting, starving, and dying—and bombs are dropped, all disagreeable things with which I have no intention of boring my contemporaries. I must merely mention them because the war had a bearing on the story I wish to tell. For the war was registered by my Aunt Milla merely as a force that began as early as Christmas 1939 to jeopardize her Christmas tree. Admittedly, her Christmas tree was unusually vulnerable.

The main attractions on my Aunt Milla's Christmas tree were glass dwarfs holding a cork hammer in their uplifted arms with a bell-shaped anvil at their feet. Under the dwarfs' feet, candles were affixed, and upon a certain temperature being reached, a hidden mechanism was set in motion and a hectic agitation was communicated to the dwarfs' arms. With their cork hammers they flailed away like crazy at the bell-shaped anvils, thus, since they were about a dozen in number, producing a concerted elfin tinkling. Furthermore: from the tip of the Christmas tree hung a red-cheeked angel in a silvery dress, and at regular intervals the angel parted its lips to whisper "Peace," and again, "Peace." The mechanical secret of this angel, obstinately guarded, became known to me much later, although at the time I had the opportunity almost every week of admiring it. In addition, of course, my aunt's Christmas tree was also bedecked with sugar rings, cookies, angel hair, marzipan figures, and—last but not least—silver tinsel; and I can still remember that properly attaching the various ornaments took a great deal of effort, requiring the participation of the entire family, so that on Christmas Eve frayed nerves cost us all our appetite, and the mood was then—as one says—dismal, except in the case of my cousin Franz, who, of course, had taken no part in these preparations and was the only one to enjoy the roast and the asparagus, the whipped cream and ice cream.

When we duly arrived, then, for a visit the day after Christmas, and risked the bold assumption that the secret of the talking angel was based on the same mechanism that caused certain dolls to say "Mama" or "Papa," the only response was mocking laughter. Now it is easy to imagine that bombs falling close by posed an extreme hazard to such a vulnerable tree. There were terrible scenes when the dwarfs fell off the tree, and once even the angel toppled to the ground. My aunt was inconsolable. After every air raid she went to endless trouble to restore the tree completely and to maintain it at least over the Christmas holidays. But even in 1940 it was already a hopeless task. Again at the risk of making myself very unpopular, I must mention in passing that the number of air raids on our city was indeed considerable, to say nothing of their violence. At any rate, my aunt's Christmas tree fell victim—the thread of my narrative forbids my mentioning other victims—to modern warfare; foreign ballistic experts temporarily snuffed out its existence.

We were all genuinely sorry for our aunt, who was a charming, gracious woman. We felt sorry that, after bitter struggles, endless arguments, after many tears and scenes, she had to agree to renounce her tree for the duration of the war.

Fortunately—or should I say unfortunately?—that was almost the only impact the war had on her. The shelter built by my uncle was bombproof; moreover, there was always an automobile ready to whisk my Aunt Milla away to areas where nothing was to be seen of the immediate effects of the war. Everything was done to spare her the sight of the appalling destruction. My two cousins were lucky enough not to have to do their war service in its most rigorous form. Johannes quickly joined his uncle's business, which played a crucial role in supplying our city with vegetables. Moreover, he had a chronic gallbladder complaint. Franz, on the other hand, although he became a soldier, was entrusted only with guarding prisoners, an assignment he utilized to render himself unpopular with his military superiors—by treating Russians and Poles as human beings. In those days my cousin Lucie was still unmarried and helped in the business. One afternoon a week she did volunteer war work at a factory that embroidered swastikas. But this is not the place to enumerate the political sins of my relatives.

Anyway, all in all there was no lack of money or food or whatever was necessary for protection, and the only thing my aunt bitterly resented was having to give up her tree. My Uncle Franz, that kindest of men, spent almost fifty years acquiring considerable merit and profit by buying up oranges and lemons in tropical and subtropical countries and selling them with a suitable markup. During the war he expanded his business to include less valuable fruits and vegetables. But after the war the gratifying produce that was his main interest was once again available, and citrus fruit became the object of keenest interest at every level. At this point Uncle Franz succeeded in regaining his former influential position, and he was able to provide the population with the enjoyment of vitamins and himself with that of a respectable fortune.

But he was almost seventy and wanted to retire, to hand over the business to his son-in-law. That is when the event occurred which at the time we smiled at but which today seems to us to have been the cause of the whole wretched sequence of events.

My Aunt Milla started in about the Christmas tree again. That was harmless enough; even the perseverance with which she insisted that everything was to be "like in the old days" merely drew smiles from us. At first there was really no reason to take it all that seriously. Although the war had destroyed so much of which the restoration caused greater concern, why—we said to ourselves—deny a charming old lady this trifling pleasure?

Everyone knows how difficult it was at that time to obtain such things as butter and bacon. But even for my Uncle Franz, who enjoyed the best of connections, it was impossible in 1945 to obtain marzipan figures, chocolate rings, and candles. It was not until 1946 that all these things could be provided. Fortunately, a complete set of dwarfs and anvils as well as an angel had survived.

I well remember the day we were invited to my uncle's home. It was in January 1947, and bitterly cold outside. But indoors it was warm, and there was no shortage of things to eat. And when the lights were put out, the candles lit, when the dwarfs began to hammer, the angel whispered "Peace," and again, "Peace," I felt transported back into an era that I had assumed to be past.

Nevertheless, this experience, although surprising, was not extraordinary. What was extraordinary was the experience I had three months later. My mother—it was now the middle of March—had sent me over to find out whether there was anything my Uncle Franz "could do": she was looking for fruit. I strolled through the streets to the part of town where my uncle lived; the air was mild, it was dusk. All unsuspecting, I walked past overgrown piles of rubble and neglected parks and, opening the gate to my uncle's garden, stopped, dumbfounded. In the quiet of the evening, the sound of singing was clearly audible, coming from my uncle's living room. Singing is a good old German custom, and there are many songs about spring, but now I could clearly hear "Holy infant, so tender and mild …"

I must admit to being confused. Slowly I approached the house, waiting for the singing to end. The curtains were drawn shut; I bent down to the keyhole. At that moment the tinkling of the dwarfs' bells reached my ear, and I could clearly hear the whispering of the angel. I didn't have the courage to intrude, and walked slowly back home. In the family, my account produced general merriment. But it was not until Franz appeared and gave us the details that we found out what had happened.

Around Candlemas, the time when in our part of the country the Christmas trees are stripped and then thrown on the garbage pile, where they are picked up by good-for-nothing children to be dragged through ashes and other rubbish, and used for various games—it was around Candlemas that the terrible thing happened. When my cousin Johannes, on Candlemas Eve, after the tree had been lit for the last time, began to detach the dwarfs from their clips, my aunt, until then such a gentle soul, set up a pitiful wail, a wail so violent and sudden that my cousin was startled, and lost control over the gently swaying tree. Then it happened: there was a tinkling and a ringing, dwarfs and bells, anvils and all-surmounting angel—everything crashed to the floor, and my aunt screamed.

She screamed for almost a week. Neurologists were summoned by telegram, psychiatrists came racing up in taxis—but all, even the most famous of them, left the house shrugging their shoulders, although also somewhat alarmed. None of them had been able to put a stop to that shrill, discordant concert. Only the strongest medication yielded a few hours of quiet; however, the dose of Luminal that can be given daily to a sixty-year-old woman without endangering her life is unfortunately rather small. But it is torture to have in the house a woman screaming at the top of her voice; by the second day the family was already totally distraught. Even the comforting words of the priest, who always celebrated Christmas Eve with the family, had no effect: my aunt screamed.

Franz made himself especially unpopular by suggesting a regular exorcism. The priest scolded him, the family was dismayed by his medieval views, and for a few weeks his reputation for brutality outweighed his reputation as a boxer.

Meanwhile everything was being tried to relieve my aunt of her condition. She refused food, did not speak, did not sleep; they tried cold water, hot foot-baths, hot and cold compresses, and the doctors searched through their reference works looking for a name for this neurosis, but could not find it.

And my aunt screamed. She went on screaming until my Uncle Franz—really the kindest of men—hit on the idea of setting up a new Christmas tree.

1952

ON CHRISTMAS EVE

Helene Stökl

It was the day before Christmas. In a woman's compartment of a railroad train which sped on from the capital out into the country and to the mountains, sat a pale young lady. The dark fur cloak closely drawn about her, the veil tied over her face, she seemed to shrink from the tumult which at every station greeted the train, and floated into the single cars, which unceasingly emptied and filled.

Half-grown boys and girls, the joy at being released from boarding school and sent home for the holidays, on their freshly reddened faces; teachers and artists, students and professors, tradesmen, merchants, office-holders, who were freed for the Christmas vacation from their callings; here a father who pants under the heavy burden of his purchases, there a grandmother, whose happy smile indicates that all the pockets of her wide, old-fashioned cloak were stuffed to the overflowing with presents for the grandchildren; here a young officer rejoicing on account of his furlough, gained with difficulty; there a little cadet, beaming in happy anticipation of being able to show himself today for the first time to his relatives, in the glory of his uniform; here a portly mother of a family, from whose ample basket came forth the most inviting Christmas odors; there a workman, the little purse with the wages saved for the holidays, in his horny hand—so they bustled and thronged and shoved, one against another, moved by the common desire to be at home as soon as possible, and to be able to spend Christmas Eve with their families.

As often as the car in which the pale young lady sat, opened to admit new travelers, she drew back farther into her corner, as if in discomfort.

She breathed a sigh of relief when at last the station was reached at which she should alight, to take from that point the branch road which, turning aside from the main line, led off diagonally straight to the mountains.

Here it was quieter. Only few stepped in, and of these few, no one into the car in which she sat. Pleased to be alone and freed from unpleasant observation, she had leaned back in the corner and had closed her eyes, when suddenly she was startled from the half slumber which had begun to take possession of her. A clear, happy child's voice had fallen shrilly on her ear. She leaned toward the window.

On the platform of a little stopping place stood a blooming young woman, in winter clothing, who held by the hand a fair-haired boy of perhaps four years, who impatiently awaiting the coming train, continually cried out, "Today is Christmas Eve! Today Papa is coming!"

The train stopped; a strong young man sprang out of the car. The next moment he had taken in his arms the boy, who, with a cry of joy, "Papa, Papa!" had freed himself from the hand of his mother. He lifted him up, he pressed him to him, he covered his face, his hair, his hands with kisses, then without letting the boy out of his arms, he turned to the young woman, who, smiling through her tears, had waited till her turn came, and pressed her also to his breast.

With a low groan the lonely woman in the car sank back in her seat. Had there not been a time when she, too, holding by the hand a fair-haired boy, had awaited, full of happy impatience, on Christmas Eve, the homecoming husband? And now!—Where was her boy, where was her husband now?

With burning, dry eyes, she looked out on the winter fields, over which the sharp wind swept, driving before it single snowflakes in wild sport.

Yes, as these flakes, so had her happiness flown away and vanished. She had once thought that she had it so securely; how had it happened that it had broken to fragments in her hand?

Before her mind the pictures of the past arose and passed slowly before her. She saw herself growing up in the house of her father, the old, rich merchant, surrounded by luxury, accustomed to flattery, and yet a poor girl, because protected by no mother.

She saw herself, hardly come to maturity, surrounded by a crowd of suitors who wished to marry the rich heiress, cold and unmoved by any attention until there stepped into her circle the one who captivated without resistance her young heart by the first glance from his sunny, happy eyes. But as high as public opinion placed the young painter, as completely as his talent freed him from the ordinary cares of life, he was not a husband whom her father would have chosen for her.

He placed no opposition to the vehement, passionate will of his daughter, but, as she followed the beloved man to his house as wife, she could not escape the conviction that when she had won a husband, she had lost a father. It grieved her, but what sacrifice would she not have made to her love! She would have given up more for his sake, that he might love her the more dearly. If she had no one but him, then he must be all to her. Wholly and completely she had given him her young heart, wholly and completely she required his in return. That the heart of a man, especially of an artist, cannot be filled singly and entirely by a woman, even if the dearest, that he knows, and must know other interests, other aims, unless he will give up his other self, that she did not know, and when the knowledge slowly dawned upon her, then she would not know it.

Her husband was accustomed to seek his recreation in a circle of congenial, joyous companions; he was pleased to think that, now that he was married, he could invite his friends to his house as a pleasant meeting place. But the free and easy manners of the young artists appealed little to the young wife; still less was she pleased by the gaiety with which her husband gave himself up to the companionship of his friends, unconcerned whether she held herself at a distance or not. She forced herself to be courteous to the guests of her husband, but they felt the restraint, and kept away. But if they did not come anymore to the house, then her husband sought them outside.

"Am I not more to you than your friends?" She begged, "give them up, for my sake." He laughed, "If I were to stay at home always with you, there would soon be an end to my art."

Yes, his art! How beautiful she had thought it, to be his muse, always by her mere presence to inspire him to splendid new creatures. But when once with restless, longing eyes, she had seated herself near him in his atelier, she was obliged to hear his friendly but decided declaration that he could work only when he was alone.

Her husband was a landscape painter, and she was spared the torment of seeing him work from models. But he possessed the beauty loving eye of an artist. He had the habit, when he went with her through the streets, of freeing himself from her arm, to walk after some beautiful girl, some comely matron, and then, returning, to praise with enthusiastic words, her beauty. His frankness should have told her how harmlessly this was meant, but she had lost, long ago, the power of unbiased judgment. She had begun to be jealous of everything that threatened to draw him away from her, of all, his friends, his art, his happy enjoyment of life, finally, also, of her child.

In a proud feeling of joy, she had been well aware of the fact that the boy whom she had given him, and whom he in overflowing paternal pride with tears of joy had pressed to his heart, gave her a double claim to his love; but this happiness remained untroubled only a short time. The child was the image of its father. As it inherited from him the color of its eyes and hair, the tone of the voice and the kind of smile, so also the child never seemed happier than in the presence of the father. Already struggling with its little arms and legs, it reached out unceasingly from the arms of the mother to the father. When it could scarcely walk, it followed its father's very footsteps or sat patiently on the stairs to await his homecoming. "Which do you love better, Papa or Mama?" she asked with trembling heart when she was alone with the child. "Both alike, and then Papa," said the child, looking at her brightly out of its large, candid eyes.

In vain she sought to gain the child's entire affection; the sunny, even kindness of the father possessed a greater attraction for the child than the passionate, unquiet tenderness of the mother.

"They care only for each other, they do not need me!" This was the tormenting thought from which she could not free herself. Her health began to suffer. "You are ill. The winter was too long and hard for you," said her husband, looking anxiously at her pale cheeks. "We will go to the mountains.

There you will grow well again." She accepted the proposition gladly. Yes, away to the mountains; perhaps it would be better there.

Deeply imbedded in a narrow valley, accessible only from one side, the mountain village that they sought out offered both a romantic and a peaceful resort, but here, too, her ardent heart found no rest.

The village was one in which her husband, before he had married, had spent many summers as a happy young artist. All knew him here, and all liked him. When he went through the village, the men stretched out their hands to him, the women brought their children to show him, the young girls from behind hedges flung roses at him, and when he decried them, fled tittering away. The pale, serious lady by his side was scarcely noticed.

With the remembrance of the old time, the old love of wandering came also powerfully over him. As before, he wandered for whole days in the mountain, filling his sketchbook as occasion presented itself, stopping where chance led him. She knew what a welcome guest he was in the most distant hut, and her heart burned when he was not with her.

He saw that she suffered, and sought to limit his excursions as much as possible. Single objects of study, as he sought them, beautiful old trees, cleft masses of rock, foaming brooks, he found in the near neighborhood of the village.

She had accompanied him a few times on these trips, but to sit for hours, while he, absorbed in his work, had not even a look for her, that her restless nature could not endure. She remained at home; so the child went with him. Leading it carefully by the hand, or, in rough places, if the little legs were tired, carrying it in his arms, so he took it with him to the spot with which he was then occupied. Playing with stones and flowers, the child waited, patient and content, however long it might be until the father had again time to turn to it.

They were too happy in these common excursions that it should not cause her anguish.

"Leave the child here," she said when he wished to take it with him the next time.

"But why?"

"You cannot take care of him while you paint. He might come to harm in the mountain."

"Nonsense!" he laughed happily. "He never stirs from my side."

"No matter, I do not wish it. The child remains here." She saw his wondering look, and added bitterly, "It is my child as well as yours! Or do you wish to deprive me of the love of my child also?"

He shrugged his shoulders, and turned aside, but after this he did not take the child with him.

And then the end came! With what terrible vividness each detail of that awful day was impressed on her mind! It was a Sunday. She had dressed herself with unusual care, in the uncertain hope that today he would stay with her. "I am going to church, will you not come with me?" she asked timidly.

"Not today, I am going to finish a sketch of the Rothe Wand, and I must have the morning light on it."

She turned away, disappointed.

"Shall you take the child with you?" he asked. "No, it stays at home with the maid."

"If you think the child is sufficiently well attended to under the care of a young thing, who is only a child herself,—" "Why not? She has nothing to do, and can pay proper attention to the child."

He made no further objections, and she went. The church was at the farther end of the village. Before she came back, more than two hours had passed. "Where is the child?" she asked the maid, who, timid and confused, stood before her.

"It's gone with the master," she stammered. "I just stepped across the street, and when I came back, the master and the child had gone away."

What? In spite of all! She pressed her lips together. Against her expressed wish, to slight and defy her, he had taken the child with him. Had it come to such a pass? In feverish impatience she waited. Noon came, and they were still away. Formerly, when he had the child with him, he had returned punctually. She let the meal be put on the table, but she could taste nothing. Inquietude drove her, restless, here and there; at last she could endure it no longer.

She took her hat and went to meet them. They could come only by this road, yes, and there they were! A little procession of boys and men, and, in front, her husband! But was that her husband? Without his hat, his clothes hanging in tatters, the blood from a wound in his forehead falling in great drops on the child in his arms!—And the child? Why did it lie so motionless! Why did it let its head hang so loosely over his arm?

She could not take a step forward. As in a fever, her teeth shut, while a cramp shook her limbs, and the cold perspiration stood out on her forehead.

Now her husband stood before her. "The child, the child!" It forced itself, gasping, from her breast. He wished to speak, but he could not. With quivering lips he bent over the child, who, stiff and white, lay in his arms. It glimmered and glittered before her eyes. Only indistinctly, as from a far distance, the murmur of the bystanders fell on her ear: "It fell over the Rothe Wand!" Then, with a shrill scream, she fell down in the dust of the road.

When she was brought to the house, they succeeded in restoring her from unconsciousness, but not from the deep apathy that had taken possession of her.

Indifferent, she looked on as they undressed the dead child and put on the little white shroud, as they laid it in the little coffin and covered it with flowers. No tear came to her eye. Silent and absorbed in herself, she sat there, only when her husband wished to approach her she turned away, shuddering.

When the hour for burial came, she roused herself. Without taking the supporting arm of her husband she followed, silent and gloomy, behind the little coffin. She saw it sunk in the earth and the mound of earth heaped above it.

Now the sexton was ready, the people, whom curiosity or sympathy had brought there, had scattered, she stood alone with her husband by the grave.

Full of ardent sympathy, he reached out his hand to her. "Why will you bear your sorrow alone, Anna?" he asked, while his voice trembled with emotion. "Am I not suffering as well as you? Is it not the child of both of us that we have buried here!"

She pushed back his hand. "You have no longer a share in the child," she said, dully.

"Anna!" he cried, amazed.

"You are guilty of his death," she pursued, with unnatural calm. "To make me ill, to grieve me, you took the child with you so that it met its death. Over this grave there is no reconciliation."

"You say I am guilty of the death of the child! I am not. Listen to me—"

She interrupted him with passionate vehemence. "And if you were not!

What does it matter, since the love between us has been dead a long time!"

"Anna, Anna! You do not know what you are saying!"

"Only too well I know. You have long ceased to love me, if, indeed, I ever possessed your love, and—I love you no more. Our paths separate."

"You are beside yourself. When you have become quieter you will think differently."

"Never!" she cried, trembling with excitement. "Have I not told you that I no longer love you? That I ceased long ago to love you? Will you compel me to live by your side with a heart that hates you? If it is on account of my property—"

He arose and walked off without once looking around.

The same evening he returned to the capital. When she followed him a few days later she did not find him. He had left a letter for her which contained the necessary arrangements to put her again in sole possession of her property, and at the same time told her of a lawyer whom he had empowered to arrange all necessary as soon as she should desire the dissolution of her marriage. He himself had gone on a journey.

Since that time nearly three years had passed, and she had not seen him again. From time to time she had read in the papers a notice of a new picture that he had painted, or, herself, had seen such a one at an exhibition, that was all.

She, too, had not remained at home. Her health was seriously affected. She had passed the first winter at Nice, the second at Meran, the intervening summer months in different parts of Baden. She had not sought a divorce. If he did not, she did not need freedom. Of what use would it be to her?

It was the first winter that she again spent in Germany. As long as she was in foreign parts, now here, now there, it had been comparatively easy to put away the thoughts she did not wish to think; now, at home, and in the old surroundings, everything powerfully recalled her to the past. To escape herself, she sought to occupy her time with works of charity; the poor and needy had always appealed to her sympathy. Sometimes she succeeded in forgetting herself in the care of others, but, in the midst of the preparations for Christmas, her strength failed her. The recollection of her vanished happiness came back with a power from which there was no escape.

How happily had she once celebrated the Christmas festival with her husband, with her child! Into the circle of light of the sparkling tree, the shadows that darkened her life never ventured. Yuletide had always been the green oasis in which her troubled heart found rest, the sacred grove unapproached by the evil spirits of jealousy, ill humor, and self-reproach, which, it is true, afterward assailed her with redoubled fury.

Every thought of the past was troubled and embittered, only the recollection of Christmas beamed bright and radiant from the gloom.

And suddenly the desire had overcome her. She would go to her child! On Christmas Day she wished to kneel by its grave; perhaps there consolation might come to her weary, despairing heart.

So she had left rich gifts for her protégés among the poor, and, on the morning of the day before Christmas, she had started, quite alone, for the mountains and the quiet village where she had to attend her child.

The train on the branch road had now reached the last station. She stepped out. From here she had still to go for half an hour over a lonely heath, overgrown with isolated pines, to the village. She took a little refreshment and started, paying no attention to the well-meant advice of the stationmaster to take an escort with her on account of the loneliness of the way. Why should she fear? Whoever is really unhappy, as unhappy as she was, does not fear. The wind blew sharply against her; she did not notice it. The physical exertion necessary to the struggle with it, on the contrary, did her good. With her cloak closely wrapped about her, she walked briskly on. She was not obliged to go quite to the village. The churchyard lay before it, a little to one side on the mountain. She was glad that it was so. It had seemed unbearable to her to have the people in the village where most of them knew her, staring at her, questioning her, perhaps even accompanying her to the churchyard. No; alone, quite alone, she wished to be with her child.

Ever more rapidly she had gone. Now she stood, struggling for breath, before the gate of the churchyard. She turned the knob; the gate was locked. As easily as she might have anticipated that the lonely churchyard, especially in winter, would not stand open, the possibility of this had never occurred to her. She looked about her. Must she then go to the village and expose herself to the curiosity of the inhabitants?

Then her glance fell on a little house that stood against the mountain a few hundred feet distant. She remembered she had heard that a woodcutter lived there with his family. The man, whose hard work often detained him for weeks in the mountains, scarcely knew her. And if he did?

She went to the house. The door was unfastened. Through a little, dark entry, she felt her way to the door. The noise, which penetrated through to her, rendered any attempt to knock a useless endeavor. She quietly opened the door and looked into the room. By a large wooden table in the center of the room sat an old, gray-haired man, whose large moustache and an empty sleeve pointed out as an old soldier, zealously busied in feeding a baby held carefully between his knees, from a bowl of food standing near him. With the rapid movement which is peculiar to a man when doing woman's work, he put the spoon in the food, lifted it out, and carried it first, to test it, to his own mouth, to which operation his moustache proved an obstacle, and then to the greedily opened mouth of the child. Then he spoke aloud to the child, and talked soothingly to it whenever he put a spoonful into the mouth of one of the two chubby children, who, with hands behind their backs and mouths open for every chance, stood nearby, while a group of older children ran and played about the room, and only a little girl, of perhaps eleven years, sat by the window attentively knitting.

"Aren't you ashamed, you little cormorant," scolded the old man, "don't you wish to give any to the rest? The sweet bread tastes good to you, too, doesn't it, Molly?" when his glance suddenly fell on the strange lady who stood, pausing, on the threshold. Astonished, he let the spoon sink into the food and attempted to stand with the child. The stranger quickly motioned to him to remain sitting.

"I wished to go to the churchyard, but it is locked. Have you no one whom you could send to the village to get the key for me?"

"The lady wants the key to the churchyard? Well, well! Tony can get it. Go, Tony," he turned to a half-grown boy who, with the other children, had gathered in curiosity around him, "run to the village for the key. Say that there is a stranger here who wants to go to the churchyard; you will bring back the key again. But don't be too long about it, hear?" The boy seized his cap and started.

"Won't the lady sit down? Lena, bring a chair!"

The old man fished carefully for the spoon which had sunk in the food, as the child on his lap would not patiently endure the interruption of its nursing.

"This screamer can't be quiet for a minute," he, confused, said apologetically, when he had recovered the spoon. "My daughter has gone to the village for bread for the holiday, and my son hasn't come home yet from his work, so the grandfather must act as nurse, whether he likes it or not."

"Are all of these your grandchildren?" asked the young lady, looking around the room with interest.

"Well, well! Seven of them. All healthy and of good appetite. Isn't it so, Molly?"

"And can the father provide bread for all?"

"Truly, it is hard work; very hard. My daughter helps as much as possible. In the summer she goes out by the day to work, if there are none too small here, but the main part falls on him."

"And is he strong?"

"He is strong, very strong, that one must admit, and good to the children beyond belief. He denies himself that he may give pleasure to them. He would have been home long ago," he pursued, winking mysteriously at the children, "but today is Christmas Eve, and probably he has something to say to the Christ Child. Now, Frank, where are you going? To meet your father? What don't you think of! Stay here, or the Christ Child won't bring you anything! They cling to their father like burs. They want to be with him all the time. In summer I can't prevent them from secretly running after him when he goes to work. It pleases him, that they know, but I can't endure it. Since I saw lying dead before me the foreign child that met its death by falling, when it had run after its father, without his knowledge, since that time I have no rest when I know that the children are not with me."

1883

NUTCRACKER AND THE KING OF MICE

E. T. A. Hoffmann

On the twenty-fourth of December Dr. Stahlbaum's children were not allowed, on any pretext whatsoever, at any time of all that day, to go into the small drawing room, much less into the best drawing room into which it opened. Fritz and Marie were sitting cowered together in a corner of the back parlor when the evening twilight fell, and they began to feel terribly eerie. Seeing that no candles were brought, as was generally the case on Christmas Eve, Fritz, whispering in a mysterious fashion, confided to his young sister (who was just seven) that he had heard rattlings and rustlings going on all day, since early morning, inside the forbidden rooms, as well as distant hammerings. Further, that a short time ago a little dark-looking man had gone slipping and creeping across the floor with a big box under his arm, though he was well aware that this little man was no other than Godpapa Drosselmeier. At this news Marie clapped her little hands for gladness, and cried:

"Oh! I do wonder what pretty things Godpapa Drosselmeier has been making for us *this* time!"

Godpapa Drosselmeier was anything but a nice-looking man. He was little and lean, with a great many wrinkles on his face, a big patch of black plaster where his right eye ought to have been, and not a hair on his head; which was why he wore a fine white wig, made of glass, and a very beautiful work of art. But he was a very, very clever man, who even knew and understood all about clocks and watches, and could make them himself. So that when one of the beautiful clocks that was in Dr. Stahlbaum's house was out of sorts, and couldn't sing, Godpapa Drosselmeier would come, take off his glass periwig and his little yellow coat, gird himself with a blue apron, and proceed to stick sharp-pointed instruments into the inside of the clock, in a way that made little Marie quite miserable to witness. However, this didn't really hurt the poor clock, which, on the contrary, would come to life again, and begin to whirr and sing and strike as merrily as ever, which caused everybody the greatest satisfaction. Of course, whenever he came, he always brought something delightful in his pockets for the children—perhaps a little man, who would roll his eyes and make bows and scrapes, most comic to behold; or a box, out of which a little bird would jump; or something else of the kind. But for Christmas he always had some specially charming piece of ingenuity provided; something which had cost him infinite pains and labor—for which reason it was always taken away and put by with the greatest care by the children's parents.

"Oh! What can Godpapa Drosselmeier have been making for us *this* time," Marie cried, as we have said.

Fritz was of the opinion that, this time, it could hardly be anything but a great castle, a fortress, where all sorts of pretty soldiers would be drilling and marching about; and then, that other soldiers would come and try to get into the fortress, upon which the soldiers inside would fire away at them, as pluckily as you please, with cannon, till everything banged and thundered like anything.

"No, no," Marie said. "Godpapa Drosselmeier once told me about a beautiful garden, with a great lake in it, and beautiful swans swimming about with great gold collars, singing lovely music. And then a lovely little girl comes down through the garden to the lake, and calls the swans and feeds them with shortbread and cake."

"Swans don't eat cake and shortbread," Fritz cried, rather rudely (with masculine superiority); "and Godpapa Drosselmeier couldn't make a whole garden. After all, we have got very few of his playthings; whatever he brings is always taken away from us. So I like the things Papa and Mamma give us much better; we keep them, all right, ourselves, and can do what we like with them."

The children went on discussing as to what he might have in store for them this time. Marie called Fritz's attention to the fact that Miss Gertrude (her biggest doll) appeared to be failing a good deal as time went on, inasmuch as she was more clumsy and awkward than ever, tumbling onto the floor every two or three minutes, a thing which did not occur without leaving very ugly marks on her face, and of course a proper condition of her clothes became out of the question altogether. Scolding was of no use. Mamma too had laughed at her for being so delighted with Miss Gertrude's little new parasol. Fritz, again, remarked that a good fox was lacking to his small zoological collection, and that his army was quite without cavalry, as his papa was well aware. But the children knew that their elders had got all sorts of charming things ready for them, as also that the Child Christ, at Christmastime, took special care for their wants. Marie sat in thoughtful silence, but Fritz murmured quietly to himself:

"All the same, I should like a fox and some hussars!"

It was now quite dark; Fritz and Marie sitting close together, did not dare to utter another syllable; they felt as if there were a fluttering of gentle, invisible wings around them, whilst a very far away, but unutterably beautiful strain of music could dimly be heard. Then a bright gleam of light passed quickly athwart the wall, and the children knew that the Child Christ had sped away, on shining wings, to other happy children. At this moment a silvery bell said, *"Kling-ling! Kling-ling!"* The doors flew open, and such a brilliance of light came streaming from the drawing room that the children stood rooted where they were with cries of "Oh! Oh!"

But Papa and Mamma came and took their hands, saying, "Come now, darlings, and see what the blessed Child Christ has brought for you."

THE CHRISTMAS PRESENTS

I appeal to yourself, kind reader (or listener)—Fritz, Theodore, Ernest, or whatever your name may chance to be—and I would beg you to bring vividly before your mind's eye your last Christmas table, all glorious with its various delightful Christmas presents; and then perhaps you will be able to form some idea of the manner in which the two children stood speechless with brilliant glances fixed on all the beautiful things; how, after a little, Marie, with a sigh, cried, "Oh, how lovely! how lovely!" and Fritz gave several jumps of delight. The children had certainly been very, very good and well-behaved all the foregoing year to be thus rewarded; for never had so many beautiful and delightful things been provided for them as this time. The great Christmas tree on the table bore many apples of silver and gold, and all its branches were heavy with bud and blossom, consisting of sugar almonds, many tinted bonbons, and all sorts of charming things to eat. Perhaps the prettiest thing about this wonder tree, however, was the fact that in all the recesses of its spreading branches hundreds of little tapers glittered like stars, inviting the children to pluck its flowers and fruit. Also, all around the tree on every side everything shone and glittered in the loveliest manner. Oh, how many beautiful things there were! Who, oh who, could describe them all? Marie gazed there at the most delicious dolls, and all kinds of toys, and (what was the prettiest thing of all) a little silk dress with many-tinted ribbons was hung upon a projecting branch in such sort that she could admire it on all its sides; which she accordingly did, crying out several times, "Oh! the lovely, the lovely, darling little dress. And I suppose, I do believe, I shall really be allowed to put it on!" Fritz, in the meantime, had had two or three trials how his new fox (which he had actually found on the table) could gallop, and now stated that he seemed a wildish sort of brute; but, no matter, he felt sure he would soon get him well in order; and he set to work to muster his new squadron of hussars, admirably equipped, in red-and-gold uniforms, with real silver swords, and mounted on such shining white horses that you would have thought they were of pure silver too.

When the children had sobered down a little, and were beginning upon the beautiful picture books (which were open, so that you could see all sorts of most beautiful flowers and people of every hue, to say nothing of lovely children playing, all as naturally represented as if they were really alive and could speak), there came another tinkling of a bell, to announce the display of Godpapa Drosselmeier's Christmas present, which was on another table, against the wall, concealed by a curtain. When this curtain was drawn, what did the children behold?

On a green lawn, bright with flowers, stood a lordly castle with a great many shining windows and golden towers. A chime of bells was going on inside it; doors and windows opened, and you saw very small, but beautiful, ladies and gentlemen, with plumed hats, and long robes down to their heels, walking up and down in the rooms of it. In the central hall, which seemed all in a blaze, there were quantities of little candles burning in silver chandeliers; children, in little short doublets, were dancing to the chimes of the bells. A gentleman, in an emerald-green mantle, came to a window, made signs, and then disappeared inside again; also, even Godpapa Drosselmeier himself (but scarcely taller than Papa's thumb) came now and then, and stood at the castle door, then went in again.

Fritz had been looking on with the rest at the beautiful castle and the people walking about and dancing in it, with his arms leaned on the table; then he said:

"Godpapa Drosselmeier, let me go into your castle for a little."

Drosselmeier answered that this could not possibly be done. In which he was right; for it was silly of Fritz to want to go into a castle which was not so tall as himself, golden towers and all. And Fritz saw that this was so.

After a short time, as the ladies and gentlemen kept on walking about just in the same fashion, the children dancing, and the emerald man looking out at the same window, and Godpapa Drosselmeier coming to the door Fritz cried impatiently:

"Godpapa Drosselmeier, please come out at that other door!"

"That can't be done, dear Fritz," answered Drosselmeier.

"Well," resumed Fritz, "make that green man that looks out so often walk about with the others."

"And that can't be done, either," said his Godpapa, once more.

"Make the children come down, then," said Fritz. "I want to see them nearer."

"Nonsense, nothing of that sort can be done," cried Drosselmeier, with impatience. "The machinery must work as it's doing now; it can't be altered, you know."

"Oh," said Fritz, "it can't be done, eh? Very well, then, Godpapa Drosselmeier, I'll tell you what it is. If your little creatures in the castle there can only always do the same thing, they're not much worth, and I think precious little of them! No, give me my hussars. They've got to maneuver backward and forward just as I want them, and are not fastened up in a house."

With which he made off to the other table, and set his squadron of silver horse trotting here and there, wheeling and charging and slashing right and left to his heart's content. Marie had slipped away softly too for she was tired of the promenading and dancing of the puppets in the castle, though, kind and gentle as she was, she did not like to show it as her brother did. Drosselmeier, somewhat annoyed, said to the parents, "After all, an ingenious piece of mechanism like this is not a matter for children, who don't understand it; I shall put my castle back in its box again." But the mother came to the rescue, and made him show her the clever machinery that moved the figures, Drosselmeier taking it all to pieces, putting it together again, and quite recovering his temper in the process. So that he gave the children all sorts of delightful brown men and women with golden faces, hands and legs, which were made of ginger cake, and with which they were greatly content.

MARIE'S PET AND PROTÉGÉ

But there was a reason wherefore Marie found it against the grain to come away from the table where the Christmas presents were laid out; and this was, that she had just noticed something there that she had not observed at first. Fritz's hussars having taken ground to the right at some distance from the tree, in front of which they had previously been paraded, there became visible a most delicious little man, who was standing there quiet and unobtrusive, as if waiting patiently till it should be his turn to be noticed. Objection, considerable objection, might, perhaps, have been taken to him on the score of his figure, for his body was rather too tall and stout for his legs, which were short and slight; moreover, his head was a good deal too large. But much of this was atoned for by the elegance of his costume, which showed him to be a person of taste and cultivation. He had on a very pretty violet hussar's jacket, all over knobs and braiding, pantaloons of the same, and the loveliest little boots ever seen even on a hussar officer, fitting his dear little legs just as if they had been painted on to them. It was funny, certainly, that, dressed in this style as he was, he had on a little, rather absurd, short cloak on his shoulders, which looked almost as if it were made of wood, and on his head a cap like a miner's. But Marie remembered that Godpapa Drosselmeier often appeared in a terribly ugly morning jacket, and with a frightful looking cap on his head, and yet was a very, very darling Godpapa.

As Marie kept looking at this little man, whom she had quite fallen in love with at first sight, she saw more and more clearly what a sweet nature and disposition was legible in his countenance. Those green eyes of his (which stuck, perhaps, a little more prominently out of his head than was quite desirable) beamed with kindliness and benevolence. It was one of his beauties too that his chin was set off with a well-kept beard of white cotton, as this drew attention to the sweet smile which his bright red lips always expressed.

"Oh, Papa, dear!" cried Marie at last, "whose is that most darling little man beside the tree?"

"Well," was the answer, "that little fellow is going to do plenty of good service for all of you; he's going to crack nuts for you, and he is to belong to Louise just as much as to you and Fritz." With which Papa took him up from the table, and on his lifting the end of his wooden cloak, the little man opened his mouth wider and wider, displaying two rows of very white, sharp teeth. Marie, directed by her father, put a nut into his mouth, and—*knack*—he had bitten it in two, so that the shells fell down, and Marie got the kernel. So then it was explained to all that this charming little man belonged to the Nutcracker family, and was practicing the profession of his ancestors. "And," said Papa, "as friend Nutcracker seems to have made such an impression on you, Marie, he shall be given over to your special care and charge, though, as I said, Louise and Fritz are to have the same right to his services as you."

Marie took him into her arms at once, and made him crack some more nuts; but she picked out all the smallest, so that he might not have to open his mouth so terribly wide, because that was not nice for him. Then sister Louise came, and he had to crack some nuts for her too, which duty he seemed very glad to perform, as he kept on smiling most courteously.

Meanwhile, Fritz was a little tired, after so much drill and maneuvering, so he joined his sisters, and laughed beyond measure at the funny little fellow, who (as Fritz wanted his share of the nuts) was passed from hand to hand, and was continually snapping his mouth open and shut. Fritz gave him all the biggest and hardest nuts he could find, but all at once there was a *crack,*

crack, and three teeth fell out of Nutcracker's mouth, and all his lower jaw was loose and wobbly.

"Ah! my poor darling Nutcracker," Marie cried, and took him away from Fritz.

"A nice sort of chap he is!" said Fritz. "Calls himself a nutcracker, and can't give a decent bite—doesn't seem to know much about his business. Hand him over here, Marie! I'll keep him biting nuts if he drops all the rest of his teeth, and his jaw into the bargain. What's the good of a chap like him!"

"No, no," said Marie, in tears, "you shan't have him, my darling Nutcracker; see how he's looking at me so mournfully, and showing me his poor sore mouth. But you're a hard-hearted creature! You beat your horses, and you've had one of your soldiers shot."

"Those things must be done," said Fritz, "and you don't understand anything about such matters. But Nutcracker's as much mine as yours, so hand him over!"

"Marie began to cry bitterly, and wrapped the wounded Nutcracker quickly up in her little pocket handkerchief. Papa and Mamma came with Drosselmeier, who took Fritz's part, to Marie's regret. But Papa said, "I have put Nutcracker in Marie's special charge, and as he seems to have need just now of her care, she has full power over him, and nobody else has anything to say in the matter. And I'm surprised that Fritz should expect further service from a man wounded in the execution of his duty. As a good soldier, he ought to know better than that."

Fritz was much ashamed, and, troubling himself no further as to nuts or nutcrackers, crept off to the other side of the table, where his hussars (having established the necessary outposts and videttes) were bivouacking for the night. Marie got Nutcracker's lost teeth together, bound a pretty white ribbon, taken from her dress, about his poor chin, and then wrapped the poor little fellow, who was looking very pale and frightened, more tenderly and carefully than before in her handkerchief. Thus she held him, rocking him like a child in her arms, as she looked at the picture books. She grew quite angry (which was not usual with her) with Godpapa Drosselmeier because he laughed so, and kept asking how she could make such a fuss about an ugly little fellow like that. That odd and peculiar likeness to Drosselmeier, which had struck her when she saw Nutcracker at first, occurred to her mind again now, and she said, with much earnestness:

"Who knows, Godpapa, if you were to be dressed the same as my darling Nutcracker, and had on the same shining boots—who knows whether you mightn't look almost as handsome as he does?"

Marie did not understand why Papa and Mamma laughed so heartily, or why Godpapa Drosselmeier's nose got so red, or why he did not join so much in the laughter as before. Probably there was some special reason for these things.

1816

CHRISTMAS IN COCHINCHINA

Joseph Roth

It occurred on one of those wonderful days, while eagerly awaiting the start of the Christmas holidays and the school break, much as I now anticipate a long journey, that the teacher said:

"Students, whoever has five pfennigs will join the class this afternoon on a trip to the World Panorama!"

I stuck two fingers up in the air and said: "I don't have five pfennigs!"

Silence reigned for a moment, as if the school principal had come to inspect. The teacher turned around, with his back toward the class and his face toward the board, as if he believed that an invisible angel with white chalk would inscribe some good advice. Something of the sort probably happened. Because after about a minute the teacher turned his face back toward the class and told me, as I remained standing, "Sit down for now!"

During recess, a school aide came to the courtyard and took me to the principal's office.

"Let's see your dirty finger!" shouted the principal. I raised both hands into the air, horizontally in front of me.

The principal leaned down a bit to examine them. But he wasn't wearing the gold-rimmed pince-nez glasses he usually had on when determined to conduct a serious investigation. I knew already that this involved something other than my dirty finger.

"You'll go to the World Panorama today without having to pay!" said the principal. Perhaps he had something else to communicate. But since the bell rang, he just muttered, "Go back to class!"

I rubbed the floorboard with my foot and left.

That afternoon at three, with dusk already looming outside the windows, we left for the World Panorama.

It was situated on a quiet, small lane and from the outside looked like an ordinary shop. A red-and-white flag hung over the glass door at which, when you opened it, a bell rang in greeting. At the entry sat a woman like a gray-haired queen selling tickets of admission. It was dark inside, warm, and very still. As soon as your eyes adjusted to the darkness, you could see a cabinet curved like a carousel and placed in the middle of the wall with viewing holes situated some eight inches apart at adult height all the way around. The viewing holes in the cabinet glimmered like cat eyes in the darkness. One sensed that the cabinet was hollow and illuminated. From there it cast a faint, mysterious shimmer that fell hazily upon the floor below. A round stool stood in front of each pair of viewing holes.

"Sit down," said the teacher, sounding as he did in the classroom, though in the darkness it was not an order, but rather a sort of gentle invitation. We moved toward the stools. I didn't quite reach because I was too short, and slightly raised the round seat to press my nose against the cabinet, my eyes against the viewing holes that were rimmed in metal.

Inside there were pictures of Cochinchina. The sky was blue, infinite, radiant. It was a kind of summery blue that looked as if it had absorbed a large portion of the shining sun, blurred it, pulverized it, and transformed it into something even more blue. One had the sense that this blue sky had to radiate, even when there was no sun. The sun itself seemed superfluous. After the second picture I no longer knew that it was December outside and that the air was filled with rainy haze. The sun blazed from the cabinet through my eyes, into my heart, and at the same time into the world. Huge palm trees stood like motionless natural towers and cast short, midday shadows that fell in dark contrast against the yellow earth. White men in pith helmets stood as if stuck, suspended in midmotion, one foot still hovering in the air so that one thought it would touch the ground once the next picture appeared. You could see half-naked native women with arousing breasts, like beautiful bronze cones that disappeared too quickly, and wearing blue loincloths that certainly would have fallen off if one could have stopped the pictures. An open-air school with a fully buttoned-up teacher from Europe teaching completely naked children. They were all squatting on the ground, each holding slate tablets in their laps. Only the teacher sat upright on a bare tree that served as a rudimentary podium. You saw fishermen and swimmers, a bicycle rider in a straw-brimmed hat, and a woman in a fluttering veil that floated white and horizontally behind her in the air, like smoke wafting behind the funnel of a steamship. As soon as a new picture appeared, something rattled inside the cabinet like in an old clock when it strikes the hour. Then a gentle, bright, lovely gong sounded. Then there was a slight tremor; the structure of the round apparatus shook as if groaning under the effort of summoning up so many foreign, distant worlds. The blue grew ever deeper, the white more radiant, the sun more golden, the green more azure, the motionless women's bodies more exciting, the naked children more graceful.

After half an hour the first picture reappeared.

Then the voice of the teacher rang out like December: "Stand up!"

Stunned, I hurried home. It was as if December were a dream that would soon come to an end and Cochinchina was the reality into which I soon had to awake. It remained like that for many years. Cochinchina stayed within me as it did in that cabinet.

A year ago, around Christmas time, I arrived in a small town. In a meager, narrow lane I spotted a sign. World Panorama was written on it. "Cochinchina!" my memory rejoiced. I went inside—no longer without paying—it cost fifty pfennigs for adults, among whom I was now oddly counted. It was almost empty. The cabinet rattled, the gong struck, just as before. But Cochinchina was no longer to be seen among the pictures. Instead you saw Switzerland. Unfortunately. In the middle of winter. Snowcapped mountain peaks. A hotel with modern comforts, with a reading room.

I leaned back. Two seats away from me sat a man. He peered, it seemed to me, with intense interest into the viewing holes. What a boring fellow! I thought, full of hatred, in the midst of the Christmas season.

When I got back outside, I became calm and reasonable. I thought that perhaps in his boyhood he had had the chance to see this very Switzerland. Without having to pay anything, before Christmas. And that, in the end, each of us have our own Cochinchina.

1929

CHRISTMAS EVE

Peter Rosegger

Year in, year out, there stood by the gray, clay-plastered wall of the stove in our living room an oaken footstool. It was always smooth and clean, for, like the other furniture, it was rubbed every Saturday with fine river sand and a wisp of straw. In spring, summer, and autumn time this stool stood empty and lonely in its corner, save when of an evening my grandmother pulled it a little forward to kneel on it and say her evening prayer. On Saturdays, too, while my father said the prayers for the end of the week, grandmother knelt upon the stool.

But when during the long evenings in late autumn the farmhands were cutting small household torches from the resinous logs, and the maids, along with my mother and grandmother, were spinning wool and flax, and all during Advent time, when old fairy tales were told and hymns were sung—then I always sat on the stool by the stove.

From out my corner I listened to the stories and songs, and if they became creepy and my little soul began to be moved with terror, I shoved the stool nearer to my mother and covertly held on by her dress; and could not possibly understand how the others still dared to laugh at me, or at the terrible stories. At last when bedtime came, and my mother pulled my little box bed out for me, I simply could not go to bed alone, and my grandmother had to lie beside me until the frightful visions had faded and I fell asleep.

But with us the long Advent nights were always short. Soon after two o'clock, the house began to grow restless. In the attics above one could hear the farm lads dressing and moving about, and in the kitchen the maids broke up kindling wood and poked the fire. Then they all went out to the threshing floor to thresh.

My mother was also up and about, and had kindled a light in the living room; soon after that my father rose, and they both put on somewhat better clothes than they wore on working days and yet not their Sunday best. Then mother said a few words to grandmother, who still lay in bed, and when I, wakened by the stir, made some sort of remark, she only answered, "You lie nice and quiet and go to sleep again!" Then my parents lit a lantern, extinguished the light in the room, and left the house. I heard the outer door close, and saw the gleam of light go glimmering past the window, and I heard the crunching of footsteps in the snow and the rattling of the house dog's chain. Then, save for the regular throb of the threshers at work, all was once more quiet and I fell asleep again.

My father and mother were going to the Rorate Mass at the parish church, nearly three hours away. I followed them in my dream. I could hear the church bell, and the sound of the organ and the Advent song, "Hail Mary, thou bright morning star!" I saw, too, the lights on the high altar; and the little angels that stood above it spread out their golden wings and flew about the church, and the one with the trumpet, standing over the pulpit, passed out over the heath and into the forests and blew throughout the whole world that the coming of the Savior was near at hand.

When I awoke the sun had long been shining into the windows; outside the snow glittered and shimmered, and indoors my mother went about again in workaday clothes and did her household tasks. Grandmother's bed, next to mine, was already made, and she herself now came in from the kitchen and helped me to put on my breeches, and washed my face with cold water, that stung me so that I was ready to laugh and cry at the same moment. That over I knelt on my stool and prayed with grandmother the morning prayer:

> In God's name let us arise
> Toward God to go,
> Toward God to take our way,

To the Heavenly Father to pray,
That He lend to us
Dear little angels three:
The first to guide us,
The second to feed us,
The third to shelter and protect us
That nothing mischance us in body or soul.

After these devotions I received my morning soup, and then came grand-mother with a tub full of turnips which we were to peel together. I sat close beside it on my stool. But in the matter of peeling turnips I could never quite satisfy grandmother: I constantly cut the rind too thick, or here and there even left it whole upon the turnip. When, moreover, I cut my finger and instantly began to cry, my grandmother said, very crossly, "You're a regular nuisance, it would be a good thing to pitch you right out into the snow!" All the while she was binding up my wound with unspeakable love and care.

So passed the Advent season, and grandmother and I talked more and more often about Christmas Eve and of the Christ child who would so soon be coming among men.

The nearer we came to the festival the greater the stir in the house. The men turned the cattle out of the stall and put fresh straw there and set the mangers and barriers in good order; the cowman rubbed the oxen till they looked quite smooth; the stockman mixed more hay than usual in the straw and prepared a great heap of it in the hayloft. The milkmaid did the same. Threshing had already ceased some days ago, because, according to our belief, the noise would have profaned the approaching Holy Day.

Through all the house there was washing and scrubbing; even into the living room itself came the maids with their water pails and straw wisps and brooms. I always looked forward to the cleaning, because I loved the turning topsy-turvy of everything, and because the glazed pictures in the corner where the table was, the brown clock from the Black Forest with its metal bell, and the various things which, at other times, I saw only at a distance high above me, were taken down and brought nearer to me, and I could observe them all much more closely and from all sides. To be sure, I was not allowed to handle such things, because I was still too clumsy and careless for that and might easily damage them. But there were moments in that eager scrubbing and rubbing when people did not notice me.

In one such moment I climbed from the stool to the bench, and from the bench to the table, which was pushed out of its place and on which lay the Black Forest clock. I made for the clock, whose weights hung over the edge of the table, looked through an open side door into the very dusty brass works, tapped several times on the little cogs of the winding wheel, and at last even laid my finger on the wheel itself to see if it would go; but it didn't. Eventually I gently pushed a small stick of wood, and as I did so the works began to rattle frightfully. Some of the wheels went slowly, others quicker, and the winding wheel flew around so fast that one could hardly see it at all. I was indescribably frightened, and rolled from the table over bench and stool down onto the wet, dirty floor; then my mother gripped me by my little coat—and there, sure enough, was the birch rod! The whirring inside the clock would not leave off, and finally my mother laid hold of me with both hands, carried me into the entrance, pushed me through the door and out into the snow, and shut the door behind me. There I stood like one undone; I could hear my mother—whom I must have offended badly—still scolding within doors, and the laughing and scrubbing of the maids, and through it all the whirring of the clock.

When I had stood there sobbing for a while and still nobody came to call me back into the house, I set off for the path that was trodden in the snow, and I went through the home meadow and across the open land toward the forest. I did not know whither I would go, I conceived only that a great wrong had been done me and that I could never go home again.

But I had not reached the forest when I heard a shrill whistle behind me. That was the whistle my grandmother made when she put two fingers in her mouth, pointed her tongue, and blew. "Where are you going, you stupid child?" she cried. "Take care; if you run about in the forest like that, Moss-Maggie will catch you! Look out!"

At this word I instantly turned around, for I feared Moss-Maggie unspeakably. But I did not go home yet. I hung about in the farmyard, where my father and two of our men had just killed a pig. Watching them I forgot what had happened to myself, and when my father set about skinning it in the outhouse I stood by holding the ends of the skin, which with his big knife he gradually detached from the carcass. When later on the intestines had been taken out and my mother was pouring water into the basin, she said to me, "Run away or you'll get splashed."

From the way in which she spoke I could tell that my mother was once more reconciled with me and all was right again; and when I went into the dwelling room to warm myself a bit, everything was back in its own place. Floor and walls were still moist, but scrubbed clean, and the Black Forest clock was once more hanging on the wall and ticking. And it ticked much louder and clearer than before through the freshly ordered room.

At last the washing and scrubbing and polishing came to an end, the house grew more peaceful, almost silent, and the Sacred Vigil was upon us. On Christmas Eve we used not to have our dinner in the living room, but in the kitchen, where we made the large pastry board our table, and sat around it and ate the simple fasting fare silently, but with uplifted hearts.

The table in the dwelling room was covered with a snow-white cloth, and beside it stood my stool, upon which, when the twilight fell, my grandmother knelt and prayed silently.

The maids went quietly about the house and got their holiday clothes ready, and mother put pieces of meat in a big pot and poured water on them and set it on the open fire. I stole softly about the room on tiptoe and heard only the jolly crackling of the kitchen fire. I gazed at my Sunday breeches and coat and the little black felt hat which were ready hanging on a nail in the wall, and then I looked through the window out at the oncoming dusk. If no rough weather set in I was to be allowed to go with the head farm servant, Sepp, to the midnight Mass. And the weather was quiet, and moreover, according to my father, it was not going to be very cold, because the mist lay upon the hills.

Just before the "censing," in which, following ancient custom, house and farm were blessed with holy water and incense, my father and my mother fell out a little. Maggie the Moss gatherer had been there to wish us all a blessed Christmastide, and my mother had presented her with a piece of meat for the feast day. My father was somewhat vexed at this; in other ways, he was a good friend to the poor, and not seldom gave them more than we could well spare; but in his opinion one ought not to give Moss-Maggie any alms whatever. The Moss gatherer was a woman not belonging to our neighborhood, who went wandering around in the forests without permission, collecting moss and roots, making fires and sleeping in the half-ruined huts of charcoal burners. Besides that, she went begging to the farmhouses, offering moss for sale, and if she did but poor business there she wept and railed at her life. Children at whom she looked were sore terrified, and many even became ill; and she could make cows give red milk. Whoever showed her kindness, she would follow for several minutes, saying, "May God reward you a thousand and a thousandfold right up into heaven!" But to anyone who mocked, or in any other way whatsoever offended her, she said, "I pray you down into the nethermost hell!"

Moss-Maggie often came to us, and she loved to sit before the house on the grass, or on the stile over the hedge, in spite of the loud barking and chain clanking of our house dog, who showed singular violence toward this woman. She would remain there until my mother took her out a cup of milk or a bit of bread. My mother was glad when Moss-Maggie thereupon gave her a thousandfold-right-up-to-heaven-may-God-reward-you; but my father considered the wish of this person worthless, whether as curse or blessing.

Some years earlier, when they were building the schoolhouse in the village, this woman had come to the place with her husband and helped at the work, until one day the man was killed at stone blasting. Since then she had worked no more, nor did she go away; but she just idled about, nobody knowing what she did or what she wanted. She could never again be persuaded to do any work—she seemed to be crazed.

The magistrate had several times sent Moss-Maggie out of the district, but she always returned. "She wouldn't always be coming back," said my father, "if she got nothing by begging in the neighborhood. As it is she'll just stay about here, and when she's old and ill, we shall have to nurse her as well: it's a cross that we ourselves have tied around our necks."

My mother said nothing in reply to such words, but when Moss-Maggie came she still gave the usual alms, and today in honor of the great feast a little more.

Hence then arose the little dispute between my father and mother, which however was at once silenced when two farmhands bearing the incense and holy water entered the house. After the censing my father placed a lighted candle on the table; today pine splinters might be burned only in the kitchen. Supper was once again eaten in the living room. During supper the head farm servant told us all manner of wonderful stories.

When we had finished my mother sang a shepherd's song. Rapturously as I listened to these songs at other times, today I could think of nothing but the churchgoing, and longed above everything to get at once into my Sunday clothes. They assured me there would be time enough for that later on; but at last my grandmother yielded to my urgent appeal and dressed me. The cowman dressed himself very carefully in his festal finery, because he was not going home after the midnight mass, but would stay in the village till morning. About nine o'clock the other farm servants and the maids were also ready, and they kindled a torch at the candle flame. I held on to Sepp, the head servant; and my parents and grandmother, who stayed at home to take care of the house, sprinkled me with holy water that I might neither fall nor freeze to death. Then we started off.

It was very dark, and the torch, borne before us by the cowman, threw its red light in a great disk on the snow, and the hedge, the stone-heaps, and the trees past which we went. This red illumination, which was broken, too, by the great shadows of our bodies, seemed very awful to me, and I clung fearfully to Sepp, until he remarked, "Look here, leave me my coat; what should I do if you tore it off my back?"

For a time the path was very narrow, so that we had to go one behind the other, and I was only thankful that I was not the last, for I imagined that he for certain must be exposed to endless dangers from ghosts.

There was a cutting wind and the glowing splinters of the torch flew far afield, and even when they fell on the hard snow crust they still glowed for a while.

So far we had gone across open ground and down through thickets and forest; now we came to a brook which I knew well—it flowed through the meadow where we made hay in summer. Then the brook had been noisy enough; today one could hear it only murmur and gurgle, for it was frozen over. We passed along by a mill where I was badly scared because some sparks flew on to the roof; but there was snow lying upon it and the sparks were quenched. When we had gone some way along the valley, we left the brook and the way led upward through a dark wood where the snow lay very shallow but had no such firm surface as out in the open.

At last we came to a wide road, where we could walk side by side, and now and again we heard sleigh bells. The torch had already burned right down to the cowman's hand, and he kindled another that he had with him. On the road were visible several other lights—great red torches that came flaring toward us as if they were swimming in the black air, behind which first one and then several more faces of the churchgoers gradually emerged, who now joined company with us. And we saw lights on other hills and heights, that were still so far off we could not be sure whether they were still or moving.

So we went on. The snow crunched under our feet, and wherever the wind had carried it away, there the black patch of bare ground was so hard that our shoes rang upon it. The people talked and laughed a great deal, but this seemed not a bit right to me on the holy night of Christmas. I could think all the while only about the church and what it must be like when there is music and High Mass in the dead of night.

When we had been going for a long time along the road and past isolated trees and houses, then again over fields and through a wood, I suddenly heard a faint ringing in the treetops. When I wanted to listen, I couldn't hear it; but soon after I heard it again, and clearer than the first time. It was the sound of the little bell in the church steeple. The lights that we saw on the hills and in the valley became more and more frequent, and we could now see that they were all hastening churchward.

The little calm stars of the lanterns floated toward us, and the road was growing livelier all the time. The small bell was relieved by a greater, and this one went on ringing until we had almost reached the church. So it was true, what grandmother had said: at midnight the bells begin to ring, and they ring until the very last dweller in the farthest valleys has come to church.

The church stands on a hill covered with birches and firs, and around it lies the little God's-acre encircled by a low wall. The few houses of the village are down in the valley.

When the people came close to the church, they extinguished their torches by sticking them head downward in the snow. Only one was fixed between two stones in the churchyard wall, and left burning.

And now from the steeple in slow, rhythmical swing, rang out the great bell. A clear light shone through the high, narrow windows. I longed to go into the church; but Sepp said there was still plenty of time, and stayed where he was, laughing and talking with other young fellows and filling himself a pipe.

At last all the bells pealed out together; the organ began to play inside the church, and then we all went in. There it looked quite different from what it did on Sundays. The candles burning on the altar were clear, white, beaming stars, and the gilded tabernacle reflected them most gloriously. The lamp of the sanctuary light was red. The upper part of the church was so dark that one could not see the beautiful painting of the nave. Mysterious shapes of men were seated in the chairs, or standing beside them; the women were much wrapped up in shawls and were coughing. Many had candles burning in front of them, and they sang out of their books when the *Te Deum* rang out from the chancel.

Sepp led me between two rows of chairs toward a side altar, where several people were standing. There he lifted me up onto a stool before a glass case, which, lighted by two candles, was placed between two branches of fir trees, and which I had never seen before when I went to church with my parents. When Sepp had set me on the stool, he said softly in my ear, "There, now you can have a look at the crib." Then he left me standing, and I gazed in through the glass. Thereupon came a friendly little woman and she whispered, "Look here, child, if you want to see that, somebody ought to explain it to you." And she told me who the little figures were. I looked at them. Save for the Mother Mary, who had a blue wrapped garment around her head which fell down to her very feet, all the figures represented mere human beings: the men were dressed just like our farm servants or the elder peasants. Even St. Joseph wore green stockings and short chamois leather breeches.

When the *Te Deum* was over, Sepp came back, lifted me from the stool, and we sat down on a bench. Then the sacristan went around lighting all the candles that were in the church, and every man, including Sepp, pulled a little candle out of his pouch, lighted it, and fastened it on to the desk in front of him. Now it was so bright in the church that one could see the paintings on the roof clearly enough.

Up in the choir they were tuning fiddles and trumpets and drums, and, just as the little bell on the door of the sacristy rang, and the priest in his glittering vestments, accompanied by acolytes and tall lantern bearers, passed over the crimson carpet to the altar, the organ burst forth in all its strength, joined by a blast of trumpets and a roll of drums.

The incense smoke was rising, and shrouding the shining high altar in a veil. Thus the High Mass began, and thus it shone and sounded and rang in the middle of the night. Throughout the offertory all the instruments were silent, only two clear voices sang a lovely shepherd song; and during the Benedictus a clarionet and two horns slowly and softly crooned the cradle song. During the Gospel and the Elevation we heard the cuckoo and nightingale in the choir, just as in the midst of the sunny springtime.

Deep down in my soul I understood it, the wonder and splendor of Christmas. But I did not exclaim with delight; I remained grave and silent; I felt the solemn glory of it all. But while the music was playing, I could not help thinking about father and mother and grandmother at home. They are kneeling by the table now in the light of the single candle, and praying; or they are even asleep, and the room is all dark—only the clock ticking—while a deep peace lies upon the forest-clad mountains, and the Eve of Christmas is spread abroad over all the earth.

The little candles in the seats were burning themselves out, one after another, as the service neared its close at last; and the sacristan went around again and extinguished the lights on the walls and altars and before the pictures with the little tin cap. Those on the high altar were still burning when a joyous march music sounded from the choir and the folk went crowding out of the incense-laden church.

When we came outside, in spite of the thick mist which had descended from the hills, it was no longer quite so dark as before midnight. The moon must have risen; no more torches were lighted. It struck one o'clock, but the schoolmaster was already ringing the prayer bell for Christmas morning.

I glanced once more at the church windows. All the festal shine was quenched, I saw only the dull red glimmer of the sanctuary lamp.

And now when I wanted to renew my hold on Sepp's coat, he was no longer there: I found myself among strangers, who talked together for a little, and then immediately set out for their several homes. My guide must be already on ahead. I hurried after him, running quickly past several people, hoping soon to overtake him. I ran as hard as my little feet were able, going through a dark wood and across fields over which such a keen wind was blowing, that warm as I otherwise was, I scarcely felt my nose and ears at all. I passed houses and clumps of trees; the people who were still on the road a short time before had dropped off little by little; I was all alone, and still I hadn't overtaken Sepp. I thought he might just as well be still behind me, but I determined to hurry straight home. Here and there I saw black spots on the road, the charcoal that folk had shaken down from their torches on their way to church. I made up my mind not to look at the bushes and little trees which stood beside the way and loomed eerily out of the mist, for they scared me. I was especially frightened whenever a path cut straight across the road, because that was a crossroad, where on Christmas Eve the Evil One loves to stand, and has chinking treasure with him with which he entices the hapless children of men to himself. It is true the cowman had said he did not believe it, but such things must be or people would not talk so much about them. I was very agitated; I turned my eyes in all directions, lest a ghost should be somewhere making for me. Then I determined to think no more of such nonsense; but the harder I made up my mind, the more I thought about it.

And now I had reached the path that should take me down through the forest and into the valley. I turned aside and ran along under the long-branched trees. Their tops rustled loudly, and now and again a great lump of snow fell down beside me. Sometimes it was so dark that I did not see the trunks until I ran up against them; and then I lost the path. This I did not mind very much, for the snow was shallow and the ground nice and level. But gradually it began to grow steep and steeper, and there were a lot of brambles and heather under the snow. The tree stems were no longer spaced so regularly, but were scattered about, many leaning all awry, many with torn-up roots resting against others, and many, in a wild confusion of up-reaching branches, lying prone upon the ground. I did not remember seeing all this on our outward journey. Sometimes I could hardly get on at all, but had to wriggle in and out through the bushes and branches. Often the snow crust gave way under me, and then the stiff heather reached right up to my chest. I realized I had lost the right path, but told myself that when I was once in the valley and beside the brook I should follow that along and so was bound to come at last to the mill and our own meadows.

Lumps of snow fell into the pockets of my coat, snow clung to my little breeches and stockings, and the water ran down into my shoes. At first all that clambering over fallen trees and creeping through undergrowth had tired me, but now the weariness had vanished; I didn't heed the snow, and I didn't heed the heather, nor the boughs that so often scratched me roughly about the face, but I just hurried on. I was constantly falling, but as quickly picking myself up again. Then, too, all fear of ghosts was gone; I thought of nothing but the valley and our house. I had no notion how long I had been astray in the wilderness, but felt strong and nimble, terror spurring me on.

Suddenly I found myself standing on the brink of a precipice. Down in the abyss a gray fog lay, with here and there a treetop rising out of it. The forest was sparser about me, it was bright overhead and the halfmoon stood in the sky. Before me, and away beyond that, there was nothing but strange cone-shaped, forest-clad mountains.

Down there in the depths must be the valley and the mill. It seemed to me as if I heard the murmur of the brook; but it was only the soughing of the wind in the forest on the farther side.

I went to right and to left, searching for a footpath that might take me down, and I found a place where I thought I should be able to lower myself by the help of the loose rocks which lay about, and of the juniper bushes. In this I succeeded for a little, but only just in time I clutched hold of a root—I had nearly pitched over a perpendicular cliff. After that I could go no farther, but sank in sheer exhaustion to the ground. In the depths below lay the fog with the black treetops. Save for the soughing of the wind in the forest, I heard nothing. I did not know where I was. If only a deer would come I would ask my way of it; quite probably it would be able to direct me, for everyone knows that on Christmas Eve the beasts can talk like men.

I got up to climb back again, but only loosened the rocks and made no progress. Hands and feet were aching. I stood still and called for Sepp as loud as ever I could. Lingering and faint, my voice fell back from the forests and cliffs. Then again I heard nothing but the soughing of the wind.

The frost was cutting right into my limbs. "Sepp! Sepp!" I shouted once more with all my might. Again nothing but the long drawn-out echo. Then a fearful anguish took possession of me. I called quickly, one after another, my parents, my grandmother, all the farmhands and maids of our household by name. It was all in vain.

I began to cry miserably.

There I stood trembling, my body throwing a long shadow aslant down the naked rock. I went to and fro along the ledge to warm myself a little, and I prayed aloud to the holy Christ child to save me.

The moon stood high in the dark heavens.

I could no longer cry or pray, I could scarcely move anymore. I crouched down shivering on a stone and said to myself, "I shall go to sleep now; it's all only a dream, and when I wake up I shall either be at home or in heaven."

Then on a sudden I heard a rustling in the juniper bushes above me, and soon after I felt that something was touching me and lifting me up. I wanted to scream, but I couldn't—my voice was frozen within me. Fear and anguish kept my eyes fast shut. Hands and feet, too, were as if lamed, I could not move them. Then I felt warm, and it seemed to me as if all the mountain rocked with me.

When I came to myself and awoke it was still night; but I was standing at the door of my home and the house dog was barking furiously. Somebody had let me slip down on the hard-trodden snow, and had then knocked loudly on the door and hurried away. I had recognized this somebody; it was the Moss wife.

The door opened, and grandmother threw herself upon me with the words, "Jesus Christ, here he is!"

She carried me into the warm living room, but from thence quickly back again into the entrance. There she set me on the bread trough, and hastened outside and blew her most piercing whistle.

She was quite alone. When Sepp had come back from church and not found me at home, and when, too, the others came and I was with none of them, they had all gone down into the forest and through the valley and up the other side to the high road, and in all directions. Even my mother had gone with them, and everywhere, all the time, had called out my name.

So soon as my grandmother believed it could no longer harm me, she carried me back into the warm room, and when she drew off my shoes and stockings they were quite frozen together and almost frozen to my feet. Thereupon she again hurried out of doors, whistled again, brought some snow in a pail, and set me barefoot down in it. Standing thus I felt such a violent pain in my toes that I groaned; but grandmother said, "That's all right; if it hurts, your feet aren't frozen."

Soon after that the red morning light shone in through the window, and one by one all the farmhands came home. At length my father, and quite last of all—when the red disk of the sun was rising over the Wechselalpe, and after grandmother had whistled countless times—came my mother. She came to my little bed, where they had tucked me up, my father sitting beside me. She was quite hoarse.

She said I ought to go to sleep now, and she covered the window with a cloth so that the sun should not shine in my face. But my father seemed to think I ought not to go to sleep yet: he wanted to know how I had got away from the servant without his noticing it, and where I had been wandering. I at once related how I had lost the path, and how I got into the wilderness; and when I had told them about the moon and the black forests, and about the soughing of the wind and the rocky precipice, my father said under his breath to my mother, "Wife, let us give God praise and thanks that he is here—he has been on the Troll's rock!"

At these words my mother gave me a kiss on the cheek, a thing she did but seldom, and then she put her apron before her face and went away.

"Well, you young Scaramouch, and how did you get home after all?" asked my father. I said I didn't know; that after a prolonged sleeping and rocking, I found myself at our door, and that Moss-Maggie had stood beside me. My father asked me yet again about this circumstance, but I told him I hadn't got anything else to say about it.

My father then said he must be off to High Mass in the church, because today was Christmas Day; and he bade me go to sleep.

I must have slept many hours after that, for when I awoke it was twilight outside, and in the dwelling room it was nearly dark. My grandmother sat nodding beside my bed, and from the kitchen I heard the crackling of the fire on the hearth.

Later, when the servants were all sitting at the evening meal, Moss-Maggie was with them at table. During the morning service she had been out in the churchyard, cowering on her husband's grave; and after High Mass my father went and found her there and brought her with him to our house.

They could get nothing out of her about the event of the night, save that she had been searching for the Christ child in the forest. Then she came over to my bed and looked at me, and I was scared at her eyes.

In the back part of our house was a room in which there were only old, useless things and a lot of cobwebs. This room my father gave Moss-Maggie for a dwelling, and put a stove and a bed and a table in it for her.

And she stayed with us. She would still very often go rambling about in the forest, and bring home moss, and then return and sit for hours upon her husband's grave; from which she could never more tear herself away to return to her own district—where, indeed, she would have been just as lonely and homeless as everywhere else. Of her circumstances we could learn nothing more definite: we could only conjecture that the woman had once been happy and certainly in her right mind; and that grief for the loss of her mate had robbed her of reason.

We all loved her, for she lived peacefully and contentedly with all and caused nobody the least trouble. The house dog alone, it seemed, would never trust her, he barked and tore furiously at the chain whenever she came across the home meadow. But the creature was meaning something quite different than we thought, all the time; for once when the chain broke he rushed to the woman, leaped whining into her bosom, and licked her cheeks.

At last in the late autumn, when Moss-Maggie was almost always in the graveyard, there came a time when, instead of barking cheerily, the dog howled by the hour together, so that my grandmother, herself very worn and weary by then, said, "You mark my words; there'll soon be somebody dying in our neighborhood now, when the dog howls like that! God comfort the poor soul!"

And a little while after that Moss-Maggie fell ill, and when winter came she died.

In her last moments she held both my father and mother by the hand and uttered the words, "May God requite you a thousand and a thousandfold, right up into heaven itself!"

1877

MARTIN'S CHRISTMAS WISH

Erich Kästner

It was nearly eight o'clock on Christmas Eve. The official weather forecast was for heavy snowfalls all over Central Europe. And now the sky was proving that the official weather forecast was very well informed, because it was indeed snowing in the whole of Central Europe.

Which meant that it was snowing in Hermsdorf. Mr. Hermann Thaler was standing at the living room window. The room was dark, because artificial light costs money, and the Thalers had to scrimp and save.

"I haven't seen such heavy snow as this for years," he said.

Mrs. Thaler was sitting on the sofa. She just nodded, and her husband wasn't expecting any answer. He was talking only to keep it from being too quiet in their apartment.

"The Neumanns are already giving their presents," he said. "Oh, and the Mildes are just lighting the candles! They have a lovely big tree. Ah, well, he's earning better again now."

Mr. Thaler looked down the street. The number of windows showing bright light grew by the minute, and the snowflakes whirled through the air like butterflies.

Mrs. Thaler moved. The old, soft sofa creaked. "I wonder what he's doing now?" she said. "In that huge school building. It must feel strange when it's so empty."

Her husband secretly sighed. "You're making things too hard for yourself," he said. "First, Jonathan Trotz is there. He seems to like Jonathan. And then there's that aristocratic little boy who broke his leg, the one with von in his surname. I'm sure they're both sitting by his bedside, having a wonderful time."

"You don't believe that yourself," said his wife. "You know as well as I do that our son isn't having a wonderful time at this moment. He's probably crept away into a corner somewhere to cry his eyes out."

"I'm sure he hasn't," Mr. Thaler replied. "He promised not to cry, and a boy like that keeps his promises." Mr. Thaler wasn't quite so sure of it as he made out. But what else was he to say?

"Promised! Promised!" said Martin's mother. "I promised him not to cry myself, but all the same I was crying even while I wrote to him."

Mr. Thaler turned his back to the window. The bright lights on their neighbors' Christmas trees were getting on his nerves. He looked at the darkness in their own living room and said, "Come along, let's have some light."

His wife rose and lit the lamp. Her eyes were red-rimmed with crying.

A very, very small fir tree stood on the round table. Mrs. Riedel, a widow who sold Christmas trees in the marketplace at this time of year, had given it to them. "For your boy Martin," she had said. So now the Thalers had a Christmas tree—but their boy, Martin, wasn't at home.

Mr. Thaler went into the kitchen, searched around for a long time, and finally came back with a little box. "Here are last year's candles," he said. "We burned them only halfway down." Then he wedged twelve halves of Christmas tree candles among the branches of the little fir. It looked really pretty at last, but that made Martin's parents only sadder than ever.

They sat side by side on the sofa, and Mrs. Thaler read Martin's letter aloud for the fifth time. She stopped at certain places and passed her hand over her eyes. When she had finished reading the letter, her husband took out his handkerchief and blew his nose hard. "To think that fate lets such things happen," he said. "A little fellow like our Martin has to find out how bad life is when you don't have any money. I hope he doesn't bear his parents a grudge for being so incompetent and poor."

"Don't talk such nonsense!" said his wife. "How can you think such a thing? Martin may still be a child, but he knows very well that being competent and being rich are very different things."

Then she fetched the picture of the blue coach drawn by six horses from her sewing table, and carefully put it under the little Christmas tree.

"I don't know anything about art," said Martin's father, "but I really like that picture. Maybe Martin will be a famous painter some day! Then we really could travel to Italy with him. Or would Spain be better?"

"Just so long as he stays healthy," said Martin's mother.

"And look at the moustache he's painted underneath his nose!"

Martin's parents exchanged melancholy smiles.

"I'm glad he didn't paint us in some showy motor car," said his mother. "The blue coach drawn by six horses is much more poetic."

"And look at those oranges!" said his father. "Oranges are never really that size. They must weigh at least four pounds each!"

"See how cleverly he cracks his whip, too," said Martin's mother. Then they fell silent again, still looking at the picture called *In Ten Years' Time*, and thinking of the little painter.

Martin's father coughed. "In ten years' time! Well, a lot can happen by then." He took some matches out of his pocket, lit the twelve candles, and put out the lamp. There was still a Christmassy glow in the Thalers' living room.

"You're a good, faithful woman," said Martin's father to his wife. "We can't afford presents for ourselves this Christmas, but we can give each other plenty of good wishes." He kissed her on the cheek. "Happy Christmas!"

"Happy Christmas!" she, too, said. Then she burst into tears, and it sounded as if she would never be able to stop crying again.

Who knows how long they would have sat on the soft old sofa like that? The candles were burning down and down. Someone was singing "Silent night, holy night" in the next-door apartment. And snowflakes were still whirling through the air outside the window.

Suddenly the doorbell rang!

Neither of them moved. They didn't want their unhappiness to be disturbed.

But then it rang again, loudly and impatiently.

Mrs. Thaler stood up and went slowly into the corridor. People wouldn't leave you in peace even on Christmas Eve!

She opened the front door, and stood there for a few seconds as if frozen rigid. Then she cried, "Martin!" The name echoed through the stairway outside.

Martin? What did she mean? Martin's father started with surprise. He went out into the corridor, and couldn't believe his eyes!

His wife had dropped to her knees in the doorway and was hugging Martin, with both her arms around him.

Then even Mr. Thaler's eyes risked shedding a tear each. He secretly wiped the two tears away, picked up the case lying forgotten on the floor and said, "My boy, for heaven's sake, how did you get here?"

✳

It was quite a long time before they all found their way back into the living room. Martin and his mother were laughing and crying both at once, and his father stammered at least ten times, "Well, what a surprise!" Then he hurried back to the front door, because in all the excitement of course they had forgotten to close it.

The first thing Martin managed to say was, "And I have the money for the return fare, too."

At last the three of them had calmed down enough for Martin to tell his parents how he came to be here instead of in Kirchberg. "I really did pull myself together," he told them, "and I didn't cry. At least, I did cry, but by then it was too late anyway. Dr. Bökh, our housemaster, noticed that something was wrong all the same. And then he gave me twenty marks. Down in the grounds, near the bowling alley. It was a present, and I'm to wish you a happy Christmas."

"Happy Christmas to you, too, Dr. Bökh!" said Martin's parents in chorus.

"And I was even able to buy some presents," said Martin proudly. Then he gave his father the cigars with the band around them and the leaf of Havana tobacco on top. And he handed his mother the knitted slippers. They were very, very pleased. "And did you like our presents?" his mother asked.

"I haven't looked at them yet," Martin admitted. So now he opened the parcel that they had sent to Kirchberg for him. He found some splendid things in it: a new nightshirt that his mother had made him herself; two pairs of woolen socks; a packet of gingerbread with chocolate icing; an exciting book about the South Seas; a drawing block and, nicest of all, a box of the best colored pencils.

Martin was delighted, and kissed both his parents.

All things considered, it was the best imaginable Christmas Eve. The candles on the tiny Christmas tree soon burned down, but then they lit the lamp. Martin's mother made coffee. His father smoked one of the Christmas cigars. Then they ate the gingerbread, and they felt happier than all the billionaires in the world put together, living and dead. Martin's mother had to try on her new slippers, and she said she had never in her life had such a wonderful pair of slippers before.

Later, Martin took a plain postcard that he had bought at the station out of his pocket, and began drawing on it. With his new colored pencils, of course.

His parents looked at each other, smiling, and then they looked at him. He drew a young man with two large angels' wings growing out of the back of his jacket. This strange man was flying down from the clouds. And below him, on the ground, stood a little boy with huge tears falling from his eyes. The man with the wings had a thick wallet in his hands and was holding it out to the boy.

Martin leaned back, narrowed his eyes in an expert way, thought for a while, and then drew some more things on the postcard: mainly a great many snow-flakes, and in the background a railway train with a decorated Christmas tree growing out of the engine of the locomotive. The stationmaster was standing beside the train, raising his arm in the signal for the train to leave. Under the picture, Martin wrote in capital letters, "A Christmas Angel Called Dr. Bökh."

His parents wrote a few lines on the back of the postcard.

"Dear Dr. Bökh," wrote Mrs. Thaler. "Our son is quite right to call you an angel. I can't draw, I can only thank you in words. Many, many thanks for the live Christmas present you have given us. You are a good man, and you deserve for all your students to grow up to be good men! With best wishes from your ever-grateful Margarete Thaler."

Martin's father growled, "You haven't left any room for me." And sure enough, he couldn't fit in much more than his name. Finally Martin wrote the address.

Then they put on their coats and went to the station together, to post the card in the overnight postbox, so that Justus would get it first thing in the morning on Christmas Day. Then they walked home again, with the boy between them, arm in arm with both his parents.

It was a wonderful walk. The sky was glittering like a never-ending jeweler's shop. It had stopped snowing, and Christmas tree lights were shining in the windows of all the buildings.

Martin stopped, and pointed to the sky. "The starlight that we see now," he said, 'is many, many thousands of years old. It takes the rays of light all that time to reach our eyes. Maybe most of these stars died out even before the birth of Christ. But their light is still traveling. So for us they still shine, although in reality they have been cold and dead for ages."

"Goodness me," said his father. His mother was astonished too. They walked on with the snow squeaking under the soles of their feet. Martin held his mother's arm and his father's arm close. He was happy.

When they were standing outside their apartment building, and his father unlocked its front door, Martin looked up at the sky once more. And at that very moment a shooting star came away from the darkness of the night, gliding silently across the sky and down to the horizon.

You can make a wish if you see a shooting star, thought the boy. And as he followed the flight of the shooting star with his eyes, he thought: then I wish my mother and father, Justus and No-Smoking, Johnny and Matz and Uli and Sebastian, too, lots and lots of happiness in their lives. And I wish the same for myself.

That was rather a long wish, but all the same he had good reason to hope that it would come true. Because all the time the shooting star was falling, Martin hadn't said a word.

And as everyone knows, that's what matters when you wish on a shooting star.

1933

THE LOAN

Wolfdietrich Schnurre

Father generally went to a lot of trouble at Christmas. It was admittedly particularly difficult at that time to get over the fact that we were unemployed. Other festivals you either celebrated or you didn't; but Christmas was something you lived for, and when it finally came you held on to it; and as for the shop windows, they often couldn't bring themselves to part from their chocolate Father Christmases even in January.

It was the dwarves and the Kasperles that did it for me particularly. If Father was there, I would look away; but that was more conspicuous than staring at them; and so gradually I started to look at the shops again.

Father was not insensitive to the shop window displays either, he just hid it better. Christmas, he said, was a festival of joy; the important thing now was not to be sad, even if one didn't have any money.

"Most people," Father said, "are just happy on the first and second days of Christmas, maybe again later at New Year. But that's not enough; you have to start the being happy at least a month before. At New Year," Father said, "you can feel free to be sad again; for it is never nice when a year simply goes, just like that. But now, before Christmas, being sad is inappropriate."

Father himself always made a big effort not to be sad around this time of year; but for some reason he found it harder than I did; probably because he no longer had a father who could say to him what he always said to me. And things would definitely also have been much easier if Father had still had his job. He would even have worked as an assistant lab technician now; but they didn't need any assistant lab technicians at the moment. The director had said that he could certainly stay in the museum, but for work he would have to wait until better times.

"And when will that be, do you think?" Father had asked.

"I don't want to upset you," the director had said.

Frieda had had better luck; she had been taken on as a kitchen help in a large pub on Alexanderplatz and had also got lodgings there straight away. It was quite pleasant for us not to be with her constantly; now we saw each other only at lunchtime and in the evening she was much nicer.

But on the whole we didn't live badly. For Frieda kept us well supplied with food and if it was too cold at home, we went over to the museum; and when we had looked at all the exhibits, we would lean against the heating underneath the dinosaur skeleton, look out the window or start up a conversation with the museum attendant about breeding rabbits.

So actually it was entirely fitting that the year be brought to an end in peace and tranquility. That was, if Father hadn't worried so much about a Christmas tree. It came up quite suddenly.

We had just collected Frieda from the pub and walked her home and lain down in bed, when Father slammed shut his book, *Brehm's Life of Animals,* which he still used to read in the evening, and called over to me, "Are you asleep yet?"

"No," I said, because it was too cold to sleep.

"It's just occurred to me," Father said, "we need a Christmas tree, don't we?" He paused for a second and waited for my answer.

"Do you think so?" I said.

"Yes," Father said, "and a proper, pretty one at that; not one of those wee ones that falls over as soon as you hang so much as a walnut on it."

At the word walnut I sat up. Maybe we could also get some gingerbread biscuits to hang on it as well?

Father cleared his throat. "God—" he said, "why not; we'll talk to Frieda."

"Maybe Frieda knows someone who would give us a tree too," I said.

Father doubted it. In any case: the kind of tree he had in mind no one would give away, it would be a treasure, a treat.

Would it be worth one mark, I wanted to know.

"One mark?!" Father snorted through his nose scornfully, "Two at least!"

"And where is this tree?"

"See," Father said, "that's just what I'm wondering."

"But we can't actually buy it though," I said. "Two marks: Where could you possibly get that money?"

Father lifted the paraffin lamp and looked around the room. I knew he was wondering whether there was anything else he could take to the pawn shop; but everything had already gone, even the gramophone; I had cried so much when the fellow behind the grille had shuffled away with it.

Father put the lamp back down and cleared his throat. "Go to sleep now; I'll have a think about the situation."

The next few days we simply hung around the Christmas tree stalls. Tree after tree grew legs and walked off; but we still didn't have one.

"Could we not—?" I asked on the fifth day, once we were leaning against the heating in the museum underneath the dinosaur skeleton again.

"Could we what?" Father asked sharply.

"I mean, should we not just try to get a normal tree?"

"Are you mad?!" Father was indignant. "Maybe one of those cabbage stalks that you don't know afterward if it's supposed to be a sweeping brush or a toothbrush? Out of the question."

But it was no good; Christmas was getting closer and closer. At first the forests of Christmas trees in the streets were still well stocked; but gradually they developed clearings, and one afternoon we watched as the fattest Christmas tree seller on Alexanderplatz, Strapping- Jimmy, sold his last little tree, a real matchstick of a tree, for three marks fifty, spat on the money, jumped on his bike and cycled off.

Now we did begin to feel sad. Not very sad; but at any rate it was enough for Frieda to furrow her brows even more than she usually did and ask us what was up.

We had got used to keeping our troubles to ourselves, but not this time; and Father told her.

Frieda listened carefully. "That's it?"

We nodded.

"You're funny," Frieda said. "Why don't you just go to the Grunewald forest and steal one?"

I have seen Father outraged many times, but never as outraged as he was this evening.

He went pale as chalk. "Are you serious?" he asked hoarsely.

Frieda was very surprised. "Of course," she said, "that's what everyone does."

"Everyone!" Father echoed, "everyone!" He stood up stiffly and took my hand. "You'll permit me," he said, "to take the boy home first before I give you the answer that deserves."

He never gave her the answer. Frieda was sensible; she played along with Father's prudery and the next day she apologized.

But it didn't make any difference; we still didn't have a tree, never mind the stately tree Father had in mind.

But then—it was December 23 and we had just taken up our usual position under the dinosaur skeleton—inspiration struck Father.

"Do you have a spade?" he asked the museum attendant, who had nodded off next to us on his folding chair.

"What?!" he yelled with a start, "Do I have a what?!"

"A spade, man," Father said impatiently, "do you have a spade?"

Yes, he had one.

I looked up at Father uncertainly. However he looked reasonably normal; only his gaze seemed a touch more unsteady than usual.

"Good," he said then, "we'll come back to your place tonight and you can lend it to us."

It was later that night before I discovered what he had planned.

"Come on," Father said and shook me, "get up."

Still drowsy I crawled over the bars of the bed. "What on earth is going on?"

"Now listen," Father said and stood in front of me, "stealing a tree, that's bad; but borrowing one, that's okay."

"Borrowing?" I asked, blinking.

"Yes," Father said. "We're going to go to Friedrichshain park and dig up a blue spruce. We'll put it in the bath in some water at home, celebrate

Christmas with it tomorrow and then afterward we'll plant it back in the same place. Well?" He gave me a piercing stare.

"A fantastic idea," I said.

Humming and whistling we set off, Father with the spade on his back, me with a sack under my arm. Every now and then Father would stop whistling and we sang in two-part harmony, "Deck the Halls" and "The First Noel the Angel Did Say." As always with such carols, Father had tears in his eyes and I too was in a very solemn mood.

Then Friedrichshain park appeared before us and we fell silent.

The blue spruce that Father had his eye on stood in the middle of a round flower bed of roses covered in straw. It was a good meter and a half tall and a model of regular growth.

As the earth was frozen only just under the surface it didn't take long at all before Father had exposed the roots. Then we carefully tipped the tree over, put it roots first into the sack, Father hung his jacket over the end sticking out, we shoveled the earth back into the hole, spread straw over the top, Father loaded the tree onto his shoulder and we went home. Here we filled the big tin bath with water and put the tree in.

When I woke the next morning Father and Frieda were already busy decorating the tree. It had been fastened to the ceiling with string and Frieda had cut a selection of stars out of tinfoil which she was hanging on its branches; they looked very pretty. I also saw some gingerbread men hanging there. I didn't want to spoil their fun; so I pretended I was still asleep. While I did, I thought about how I could repay them for their kindness. Eventually it occurred to me: Father had borrowed a Christmas tree, why shouldn't I also manage to get a loan of our pawned gramophone for the holidays? I acted like I had just woken up, admired the tree in seemly fashion and then I got dressed and went out.

The pawnbroker was a horrible person, even the first time we were there and Father had given him his coat. I would have happily given him something else too; but now it was necessary to be friendly to him.

I also made a great effort. I told him a story of two grandmothers and "especially at Christmas" and "enjoying the old days one more time" and so on, and suddenly the pawnbroker struck out and clouted me one and said quite calmly, "I don't care how much you fib otherwise; but at Christmas you tell the truth, got it?" Then he shuffled into the next room and brought out the gramophone. "But woe betide you if you break anything! And only for three days! And only because it's you."

I made a bow, so low that I nearly bumped my head against my kneecap; then I took the turntable under one arm, the horn under the other and ran back home.

First I hid both bits in the wash-kitchen. I did have to let Frieda in on the secret, for she had the records; but Frieda kept mum.

Frieda's boss, the landlord of the pub, had invited us for lunch. There was impeccable noodle soup followed by mashed potato and giblets. We ate until we were unrecognizable; afterward in order to save coal we went to the museum and the dinosaur skeleton for a while; and in the afternoon Frieda came and collected us.

At home we lit a fire. Then Frieda brought out a huge bowl full of the leftovers of the giblets, three bottles of red wine and a square meter of *Bienenstich* cake. Father put his volume of *Brehm's Life of Animals* on the table for me, and the moment he wasn't looking I ran down to the washkitchen and brought up the gramophone and told Father to face the other way.

He did as he was told; Frieda spread out the records and put the lights on, and I fixed the horn and wound the gramophone.

"Can I turn around yet?" Father asked; when Frieda had switched the light off he could stand it no longer.

"Wait a second," I said, "this damn horn—I can't get it to stay put!" Frieda coughed.

"What horn do you mean?" Father asked.

But then it started. It was "O Come Little Children;" it crackled a bit and the record obviously had a scratch, but that didn't matter. Frieda and I sang along and then Father turned around. First he swallowed and rubbed his nose, but then he cleared his throat and sang along too. When the record was finished we shook hands and I told Father how I'd managed to get the gramophone. He was thrilled. "Well!" he kept on saying to Frieda and nodded at me as he did so, "well!"

It turned into a very lovely Christmas evening. First we sang and played all the records through; then we played them again without singing; then Frieda sang along with all of the records on her own; then she sang with Father again, and then we ate and finished the wine and after that we made some music; then we walked Frieda home and we went to bed too.

The next morning the tree stayed standing in all its finery. I was allowed to lie in bed and Father played gramophone music all night and whistled the harmony.

Then, the following night, we took the tree out of the bath, put it in the sack, still decorated with tinfoil stars, and took it back to Friedrichshain park. Here we planted it back in the round rose bed. Then we stamped the earth firm and went home. In the morning I took the gramophone away too.

We visited the tree frequently; the roots grew back again. The tinfoil stars hung in its branches for quite a while, some even until spring.

I went to see the tree again a few months ago. It's now a good two stories high and has the circumference of a medium-sized factory chimney. It seems strange to think that we once invited it into our one-room apartment.

1958

O TANNENBAUM

Ernst Anschütz

O evergreen, O evergreen,
    How are thy leaves so verdant;
Not only in the summer time
But e'en in winter is thy prime;
    O evergreen, O evergreen,
    How are thy leaves so verdant?

O evergreen, O evergreen,
    We sing in happy measure.
Thy praise who dost our Christmas greet
With verdure fair and mem'ries sweet;
    O evergreen, O evergreen,
    Tree of unfailing treasure.

O evergreen, O evergreen,
    Thy garb unfading showeth
The flower of joy abut my door,
Good cheer that faileth nevermore.
    O evergreen, O evergreen,
    My heart thy lesson knoweth.

1824

ERNST ANSCHÜTZ (1780–1861) is best known for his reworking of August Zarnack's 1820 love poem, "O Tannenbaum," into the Christmas carol known today. Anschütz was also a composer, music teacher, and choirmaster, who set to music, among many other poems, Wilhelm Hey's classic Christmas carol "Alle Jahre wieder," although his is not the most common melody.

HEINRICH BÖLL (1917–1985) was injured four times as a soldier in World War II, and taken prisoner in 1945. These early experiences shaped his long career as an antiwar novelist critical of authority and devoted to individual experience, usually writing in the first person. Several of Böll's novels were adapted for film, and he won the Nobel Prize for Literature in 1972.

ILSE FRAPAN (1849–1908) was the pseudonym of Ilse Levien, beloved for her children's literature and plays. She married Armenian author Iwan Akunian and took his name, but lived from 1883 with the artist Emma Mandelbaum, with whom she made a death pact after learning of a terminal illness in 1908.

JOHANN WOLFGANG VON GOETHE (1749–1832) is widely considered the greatest poet of the German language. Goethe was born to wealth in Frankfurt and raised to nobility in Weimar, where he settled. He became renowned in his lifetime both for his poetry and his first two novels, *The Sorrows of Young Werther* and *Wilhelm Meister's Apprenticeship*.

THE BROTHERS GRIMM, JACOB LUDWIG KARL GRIMM (1785–1863) and WILHELM CARL GRIMM (1786–1859) were the foremost among many German collectors and authors of folktales. The brothers spent their lives together, from their childhood in Hesse to their careers in civil parliament and at the University of Berlin. In their last years, the Grimms devoted their time to work on a dictionary of the German language, which was left unfinished.

HEINRICH HEINE (1797–1856) was born Harry Heine to a Jewish family in Düsseldorf. Heine failed in an early business venture as well as his legal education. Heine's 1827 *Book of Songs* was well received and earned him some celebrity, but his great body of critical prose was largely ignored. After the July Revolution of 1830, Heine moved to Paris, where he stayed for the rest of his life.

HERMANN HESSE (1877–1962) grew up well educated by his family, which included missionaries to India and orientalists studying the same nation. Hesse began his career as a poet and novelist in the Romantic tradition, but after his own journey to India he too focused his creative output on an understanding of Indian life and religion. His most well-known works, the novels *Siddhartha* and *Steppenwolf*, evince this familial fascination. Hesse received the Nobel Prize in Literature in 1946.

E.T.A. HOFFMANN (1776–1822) was born Ernst Theodor Wilhelm Hoffmann, but changed his third name to Amadeus in homage to Wolfgang Amadeus Mozart, whom he greatly admired. Hoffmann drew, painted portraits, and composed music, but he found the most success in writing, first music criticism, and then, to great acclaim, short fiction and novels.

ERICH KÄSTNER (1899–1974) was a greatly successful children's author, best known to this day for his book *Emil and the Detectives*. Several of his novels have been adapted for screen. Kästner was nominated four times for the Nobel Prize in Literature and was awarded the international Hans Andersen Prize for children's literature in 1961.

THOMAS MANN (1875–1955) was among the most renowned novelists of the twentieth century and received the 1929 Nobel Prize in Literature. *Buddenbrooks*, his first novel, published in 1901, found great success in Germany.

Mann, however, was deprived of German citizenship in 1936 by the Nazi regime and eventually sought refuge in the United States before living his final years in Switzerland.

RAINER MARIA RILKE (1875–1926) was the author of twelve volumes of poetry, including the world-renowned *Book of Hours*, *Duino Elegies*, and *Sonnets to Orpheus*, as well as the novel *The Notebooks of Malte Laurids Brigge* and the book of correspondence *Letters to a Young Poet*. Rilke is one of the most influential poets of the twentieth century, having inspired W. H. Auden, W. S. Merwin, and John Ashbery, as well as novelists like Thomas Pynchon.

PETER ROSEGGER (1843–1918) was born in rural poverty and began to write while a tailor's apprentice. Along with German novels including *Manuscripts of a Forest-School Master* and a collection of stories for "the young" (people between fifteen and seventy years old, by Rosegger's definition), Rosegger also wrote poems and stories in his native Styrian dialect.

JOSEPH ROTH (1894–1939) was born in Brody in Eastern Ukraine, just west of Russia, but studied in and fought for Austria during World War I. The details of his biography are unclear due to Roth's tendency to distort his experiences when describing them. He wrote his greatest work, seven novels including *Job* and *Radetzky March*, in the 1920s and early 1930s, and became a great expatriate writer in Paris from 1933 until his death in 1939.

ARTHUR SCHNITZLER (1862–1931) lived his whole life in Vienna, where he studied and practiced medicine, following in the footsteps of his father, a successful Jewish doctor, before making a career in writing. He was most successful as a playwright, although he was also acclaimed for his novellas, including *Dying, Fräulein Else*, and *Dream Story*.

WOLFDIETRICH SCHNURRE (1920–1989) grew up in Frankfurt and moved to Berlin in 1928. He was conscripted and fought for the Nazi Wehrmacht in World War II, ending in a penal battalion for attempted desertion.

After his return to Berlin in 1946 Schnurre co-founded *Gruppe 47*, but left the literary group in 1951. A perennial outsider and bitter critic, Schnurre became best known for his aphoristic short stories.

PETER STAMM (1963–) is the Swiss author of eleven novels, along with several short story collections, plays, and radio dramas. Several of his works have been translated into English. He has received several German language literary prizes, and was short-listed for the 2013 Man Booker International Prize for his full body of work.

HELENE STÖKL (1845–1929) was born Helene Boeckel and wrote under the pseudonym Constanze von Franken, Joconde. Stökl was a schoolteacher as well as a children's writer known for her *Backfischromane* (novels for teenage girls) and her *Handbook of Good Style and Breeding*.

MARTIN SUTER (1948–) is a novelist, screenwriter, and newspaper columnist born in Zurich, Switzerland. He has written a dozen novels, many of them bestsellers in Europe and translated into thirty-two languages, including *The Last Weynfeldt*, as well as *Allmen and the Dragonflies* and its sequel *Allmen and the Pink Diamond*. Suter lives with his family in Zurich.

KURT TUCHOLSKY (1890–1935) was a journalist best known in his time for his satirical poems and songs. As a Jewish left-wing writer, Tucholsky had his citizenship revoked in 1933, and his books burned by the Nazi party. He took his own life near Gothenburg, Sweden, in 1935.

"Martin's Christmas Wish"
translated by Anthea Bell

"The Christmas Box"
translated by Edgar Alfred Browning

"O Tannenbaum"
translated by W. H. Dawson

"Nutcracker and the King of Mice"
translated by Major Alex Ewing

"Christmas"
"Interview with Santa Claus"
"Every Year Once Again—The Client Gift"
"Advent"
translated by Henry N. Gifford

"In the Outer Suburbs"
translated by Michael Hofmann

"Christmas Eve"
translated by Maude Egerton King

"Christmas with the Buddenbrooks"
From the novel *Buddenbrooks: The Decline of a Family*
translated by John E. Woods

"The Separation"
From the novel *A Christmas Story*
translated by Helen A. Macdonell

"The Loan"
From the novel *Als Vaters Bart noch rot war*
translated by Lyn Marven

"Berlin at Christmastide"
From *Letters from Berlin*
translated by Elizabeth A. Sharp

"The Elves and the Shoemaker"
translated by Edgar Taylor

"Christmas Not Just Once a Year"
translated by Leila Vennewitz

"On Christmas Eve"
translated by Helen E. Wilson

"After Christmas"
"Christmas Shopping"
From the play *Anatol*
"Christmas in Cochinchina"
translated by Michael Z. Wise

A VERY SCANDINAVIAN CHRISTMAS

The best Scandinavian holiday stories including classics by Hans Christian Andersen, Nobel Prize winner Selma Lagerlöf, August Strindberg as well as popular Norwegian author Karl Ove Knausgaard. These Nordic tales—coming from the very region where much traditional Christmas imagery originates—convey a festive spirit laden with lingonberries, elks, gnomes and aquavit in abundance. A smorgasbord of unexpected literary gifts sure to provide plenty of pleasure and *hygge*, that specifically Scandinavian blend of coziness and contentment.

A VERY FRENCH CHRISTMAS

A continuation of the very popular Very Christmas Series, this collection brings together the best French Christmas stories of all time in an elegant and vibrant collection featuring classics by Guy de Maupassant and Alphonse Daudet, plus stories by the esteemed twentieth century author Irène Némirovsky and contemporary writers Dominique Fabre and Jean-Philippe Blondel. With a holiday spirit conveyed through sparkling Paris streets, opulent feasts, wandering orphans, flickering desire, and more than a little wine, this collection proves that the French have mastered Christmas.

A VERY ITALIAN CHRISTMAS

This volume brings together the best Italian Christmas stories of all time in a fascinating collection featuring classic tales and contemporary works. With writing that dates from the Renaissance to the present day, from Boccaccio to Pirandello, as well as Anna Maria Ortese, Natalia Ginzburg and Nobel laureate Grazia Deledda, this choice selection delights and intrigues. Like everything the Italians do, this is Christmas with its very own verve and flair, the perfect literary complement to a *Buon Natale italiano*.

A VERY RUSSIAN CHRISTMAS

This is Russian Christmas celebrated in supreme pleasure and pain by the greatest of writers, from Dostoevsky and Tolstoy to Chekhov and Teffi. The dozen stories in this collection will satisfy every reader, and with their wit, humor, and tenderness, packed full of sentimental songs, footmen, whirling winds, solitary nights, snow drifts, and hopeful children, the collection proves that Nobody Does Christmas Like the Russians.

EXPOSED by Jean-Philippe Blondel

A dangerous intimacy emerges between a French teacher and a former student who has achieved art world celebrity. The painting of a portrait upturns both their lives. Jean-Philippe Blondel, author of the bestselling novel *The 6:41 to Paris*, evokes an intimacy of dangerous intensity in a stunning tale about aging, regret and moving ahead into the future.

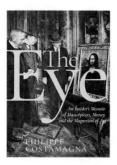

THE EYE by Philippe Costamagna

It's a rare and secret profession, comprising a few dozen people around the world equipped with a mysterious mixture of knowledge and innate sensibility. Summoned to Swiss bank vaults, Fifth Avenue apartments, and Tokyo storerooms, they are entrusted by collectors, dealers, and museums to decide if a coveted picture is real or fake and to determine if it was painted by Leonardo da Vinci or Raphael. *The Eye* lifts the veil on the rarified world of connoisseurs devoted to the authentication and discovery of Old Master artworks.

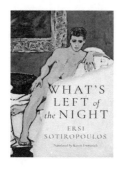

WHAT'S LEFT OF THE NIGHT by Ersi Sotiropoulos

Constantine Cavafy arrives in Paris in 1897 on a trip that will deeply shape his future and push him toward his poetic inclination. With this lyrical novel, tinged with an hallucinatory eroticism that unfolds over three unforgettable days, celebrated Greek author Ersi Sotiropoulos depicts Cavafy in the midst of a journey of self-discovery across a continent on the brink of massive change. A stunning portrait of a budding author—before he became C.P. Cavafy, one of the 20th century's greatest poets—that illuminates the complex relationship of art, life, and the erotic desires that trigger creativity.

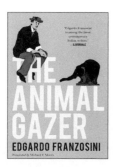

THE ANIMAL GAZER by Edgardo Franzosini

A hypnotic novel inspired by the strange and fascinating life of sculptor Rembrandt Bugatti, brother of the fabled automaker. Bugatti obsessively observes and sculpts the baboons, giraffes, and panthers in European zoos, finding empathy with their plight and identifying with their life in captivity. Rembrandt Bugatti's work, now being rediscovered, is displayed in major art museums around the world and routinely fetches large sums at auction. Edgardo Franzosini recreates the young artist's life with intense lyricism, passion, and sensitivity.

ALLMEN AND THE DRAGONFLIES by Martin Suter

Johann Friedrich von Allmen has exhausted his family fortune by living in Old World grandeur despite present-day financial constraints. Forced to downscale, Allmen inhabits the garden house of his former Zurich estate, attended by his Guatemalan butler, Carlos. This is the first of a series of humorous, fast-paced detective novels devoted to a memorable gentleman thief. A thrilling art heist escapade infused with European high culture and luxury that doesn't shy away from the darker side of human nature.

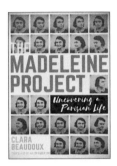

THE MADELEINE PROJECT by Clara Beaudoux

A young woman moves into a Paris apartment and discovers a storage room filled with the belongings of the previous owner, a certain Madeleine who died in her late nineties, and whose treasured possessions nobody seems to want. In an audacious act of journalism driven by personal curiosity and humane tenderness, Clara Beaudoux embarks on *The Madeleine Project*, documenting what she finds on Twitter with text and photographs, introducing the world to an unsung 20th century figure.

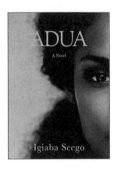

ADUA by Igiaba Scego

Adua, an immigrant from Somalia to Italy, has lived in Rome for nearly forty years. She came seeking freedom from a strict father and an oppressive regime, but her dreams of film stardom ended in shame. Now that the civil war in Somalia is over, her homeland calls her. She must decide whether to return and reclaim her inheritance, but also how to take charge of her own story and build a future.

IF VENICE DIES by Salvatore Settis

Internationally renowned art historian Salvatore Settis ignites a new debate about the Pearl of the Adriatic and cultural patrimony at large. In this fiery blend of history and cultural analysis, Settis argues that "hit-and-run" visitors are turning Venice and other landmark urban settings into shopping malls and theme parks. This is a passionate plea to secure the soul of Venice, written with consummate authority, wide-ranging erudition and élan.

THE MADONNA OF NOTRE DAME by Alexis Ragougneau

Fifty thousand people jam into Notre Dame Cathedral to celebrate the Feast of the Assumption. The next morning, a beautiful young woman clothed in white kneels at prayer in a cathedral side chapel. But when someone accidentally bumps against her, her body collapses. She has been murdered. This thrilling novel illuminates shadowy corners of the world's most famous cathedral, shedding light on good and evil with suspense, compassion and wry humor.

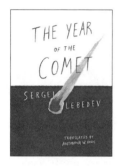

THE YEAR OF THE COMET by Sergei Lebedev

A story of a Russian boyhood and coming of age as the Soviet Union is on the brink of collapse. Lebedev depicts a vast empire coming apart at the seams, transforming a very public moment into something tender and personal, and writes with stunning beauty and shattering insight about childhood and the growing consciousness of a boy in the world.

THE LAST WEYNFELDT by Martin Suter

Adrian Weynfeldt is an art expert in an international auction house, a bachelor in his mid-fifties living in a grand Zurich apartment filled with costly paintings and antiques. Always correct and well-mannered, he's given up on love until one night—entirely out of character for him—Weynfeldt decides to take home a ravishing but unaccountable young woman and gets embroiled in an art forgery scheme that threatens his buttoned up existence. This refined page-turner moves behind elegant bourgeois facades into darker recesses of the heart.

THE LAST SUPPER by Klaus Wivel

Alarmed by the oppression of 7.5 million Christians in the Middle East, journalist Klaus Wivel traveled to Iraq, Lebanon, Egypt, and the Palestinian territories to learn about their fate. He found a minority under threat of death and humiliation, desperate in the face of rising Islamic extremism and without hope their situation will improve. An unsettling account of a severely beleaguered religious group living, so it seems, on borrowed time. Wivel asks, Why have we not done more to protect these people?

THE 6:41 TO PARIS by Jean-Philippe Blondel

Cécile, a stylish 47-year-old, has spent the weekend visiting her parents outside Paris. By Monday morning, she's exhausted. These trips back home are stressful and she settles into a train compartment with an empty seat beside her. But it's soon occupied by a man she recognizes as Philippe Leduc, with whom she had a passionate affair that ended in her brutal humiliation 30 years ago. In the fraught hour and a half that ensues, Cécile and Philippe hurtle towards the French capital in a psychological thriller about the pain and promise of past romance.

ON THE RUN WITH MARY by Jonathan Barrow

Shining moments of tender beauty punctuate this story of a youth on the run after escaping from an elite English boarding school. At London's Euston Station, the narrator meets a talking dachshund named Mary and together they're off on escapades through posh Mayfair streets and jaunts in a Rolls-Royce. But the youth soon realizes that the seemingly sweet dog is a handful; an alcoholic, nymphomaniac, drug-addicted mess who can't stay out of pubs or off the dance floor. *On the Run with Mary* mirrors the horrors and the joys of the terrible 20th century.

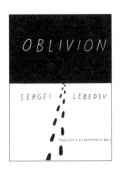

OBLIVION by Sergei Lebedev

In one of the first 21st century Russian novels to probe the legacy of the Soviet prison camp system, a young man travels to the vast wastelands of the Far North to uncover the truth about a shadowy neighbor who saved his life, and whom he knows only as Grandfather II. Emerging from today's Russia, where the ills of the past are being forcefully erased from public memory, this masterful novel represents an epic literary attempt to rescue history from the brink of oblivion.

MOVING THE PALACE by Charif Majdalani

A young Lebanese adventurer explores the wilds of Africa, encountering an eccentric English colonel in Sudan and enlisting in his service. In this lush chronicle of far-flung adventure, the military recruit crosses paths with a compatriot who has dismantled a sumptuous palace and is transporting it across the continent on a camel caravan. This is a captivating modern-day Odyssey in the tradition of Bruce Chatwin and Paul Theroux.

GUYS LIKE ME by Dominique Fabre

Dominique Fabre, born in Paris and a life-long resident of the city, exposes the shadowy, anonymous lives of many who inhabit the French capital. In this quiet, subdued tale, a middle-aged office worker, divorced and alienated from his only son, meets up with two childhood friends who are similarly adrift. He's looking for a second act to his mournful life, seeking the harbor of love and a true connection with his son. Set in palpably real Paris streets that feel miles away from the City of Light, a stirring novel of regret and absence, yet not without a glimmer of hope.

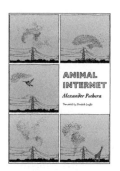

ANIMAL INTERNET by Alexander Pschera

Some 50,000 creatures around the globe—including whales, leopards, flamingoes, bats and snails—are being equipped with digital tracking devices. The data gathered and studied by major scientific institutes about their behavior will warn us about tsunamis, earthquakes and volcanic eruptions, but also radically transform our relationship to the natural world. Contrary to pessimistic fears, author Alexander Pschera sees the Internet as creating a historic opportunity for a new dialogue between man and nature.

KILLING AUNTIE by Andrzej Bursa

A young university student named Jurek, with no particular ambitions or talents, finds himself with nothing to do. After his doting aunt asks the young man to perform a small chore, he decides to kill her for no good reason other than, perhaps, boredom. This short comedic masterpiece combines elements of Dostoevsky, Sartre, Kafka, and Heller, coming together to produce an unforgettable tale of murder and—just maybe—redemption.

I CALLED HIM NECKTIE by Milena Michiko Flašar

Twenty-year-old Taguchi Hiro has spent the last two years of his life living as a hikikomori—a shut-in who never leaves his room and has no human interaction—in his parents' home in Tokyo. As Hiro tentatively decides to reenter the world, he spends his days observing life from a park bench. Gradually he makes friends with Ohara Tetsu, a salaryman who has lost his job. The two discover in their sadness a common bond. This beautiful novel is moving, unforgettable, and full of surprises.

New Vessel Press

To purchase these titles and for more information please visit newvesselpress.com.